Puck Around And Find Out

Okie Icebreakers

Annika Rhyder

Published by Annika Rhyder, 2023.

PUCK AROUND AND FIND OUT

First edition. June 25, 2023.

ISBN: 979-8223257400

Written by Annika Rhyder.

Blurb

She's shooting for his heart. He's defending his line. Who will score?

At 35, Daniel Crowe is a seasoned warrior in the youthful arena of the Okie Icebreakers. Making a comeback from a career-threatening injury, his focus is solely on the challenging path back to his former glory in professional hockey. However, in the heart-pounding symphony of the game and the shattering clashes on the ice, a captivating diversion emerges—one that tempts and unsettles him in ways no game ever has. Evie Manning, a vibrant 20-year-old siren and daughter of Crowe's formidable coach, is as impassioned about hockey as she is about the gruff player she has secretly adored for years. With Crowe back on home ice, Evie wastes no time and launches a daring game of seduction, determined to conquer the age gap and the professional boundaries standing between them.

Crowe's initial resistance crumbles under Evie's persistent charm and seductive allure. The lines blur, rules are broken, and their clandestine affair soon becomes public knowledge, sending shockwaves through their families, the team, and the public eye. Caught in a whirlwind of scandal and scrutiny, Crowe and Evie must not only fight for their love but also Crowe's redemption on the ice.

A grumpy/sunshine age-gap romance.

Chapter 1: Return to the Rink

A chill settled deep in Daniel Crowe's bones as he stepped onto the immaculate ice of the rink, a sensation more profound than the biting frost in the air. The harsh glare of overhead lights, their reflection off the polished surface beneath his blades, brought a gleam to his eyes. He stood there, a figure in his mid-thirties, battle-worn and slightly out of place amidst the thrum of youthful energy that pervaded the space.

The scrape and crunch of skate blades against the ice echoed around the cavernous arena. His teammates whirled and swooped, exuding exuberance and vitality. A tangible cloud of anticipation and anxiety permeated the air, laced with the sharp scent of cold and the musk of athletic determination.

On the sideline, Coach Van Manning loomed like a grizzled sentinel. Arms crossed, eyes unreadable behind a weathered brow and graying beard, he observed Crowe with a mixture of skepticism and hope. His mouth set in a hard line, a physical manifestation of his silent doubts regarding Crowe's capacity to rebound from last season's career-threatening injury. Crowe could feel it pouring off the man.

Crowe, acutely aware of the coach's scrutiny, shifted his focus to the cool, icy surface beneath him. His hand swept over the puck, tracing the rough edges and smooth curves—its familiar shape a beacon in the storm of his uncertainty. He could hear the soft whir of the overhead ventilation, the distant chatter of his teammates, and the rhythmic thud of his heart against his ribcage.

Pushing off with a forceful stride, Crowe surrendered to the graceful dance of the game. His body, though scarred and slightly resistant, recalled the rhythm of movement, the song of the ice. The whirring crowd and the booming announcements over the PA system became a backdrop to his personal symphony. A sheen of sweat coated his brow, the burn in his muscles a constant reminder of his physical reality.

Circling the rink, Crowe grappled with the unshakeable notion that this might be his last chance. Each stride, each turn, each hit reverberated with the echoes of a career that had been his life's cornerstone. The puck in his grasp felt like the embodiment of his dreams, teetering on the edge of a precipice.

Despite his lingering apprehension, Crowe moved with a dancer's grace and a warrior's determination. He weaved through his teammates, shot the puck with a precision born of years of practice, and accepted the brutal hits as part of the game. His focus narrowed to the ice, the puck, and the goal—a beacon at the end of a path riddled with obstacles.

As the practice session ended, Crowe skated off the ice, his breath creating misty clouds in the freezing air. The taste of exertion laid heavy on his tongue, the sting of cold air in his lungs a vivid reminder of the life he'd fought to regain. Amidst the doubts and uncertainty, the ice rink stood as a fortress of familiarity, a testament to the past, and perhaps, the key to his future.

Crowe's gaze shifted across the ice, a silent observer to the whirlwind of activity. Each pass, each shot, resonated with a primal familiarity that spoke of countless hours spent in this very arena. The cold, crisp air filled his lungs, cleansing, invigorating, while the thin veneer of sweat coating his skin offered a stark contrast to the icy temperature of the rink.

As the final whistle blew, signifying the end of the practice session, Crowe skated over to join the rest of his team who were already gathered by the boards, slapping their sticks against the ice in an age-old hockey salute.

"Hey, Old Man," said Ryan, a lopsided grin on his youthful face. "You're not going to start needing a walker to get around the ice, are you?"

Laughter rippled through the team, and even Crowe found himself suppressing a smile. "With the way you lot have been playing, I could use a walker and still outpace you."

Tyler, the team's usually quiet goalie, chimed in, "Crowe, you keep saying that, and we'll have to arrange a race to put that claim to the test."

The banter continued, a volley of jests and jibes tossed back and forth with good-natured ease. Carter, the ambitious new forward, tried to get a rise out of Andrei, their stoic Russian teammate, while Liam, the gentle giant, chuckled warmly at the younger man's attempts.

Meanwhile, Dominic, Crowe's closest friend on the team, clapped him on the shoulder. "Good to have you back, Crowe. The ice missed you."

Crowe nodded, a shadow of appreciation in his eyes. He took in the camaraderie, the easy rapport, and the simple joy of being part of a team. This was what he'd missed during his time away—the thrill of the game, yes, but also this sense of belonging, of being a part of something greater than himself.

Despite the lingering specter of his injury and the uncertainty of his future, for that one fleeting moment, everything felt as it should.

The noise and banter around him quieted to a low hum as Crowe's gaze fell upon a familiar figure behind the frosted glass. Evie. Her green eyes, alight with mirth and something more elusive, met his. The sight of her elicited a rush of warmth that clashed with the frigid air around him, heating his blood and stirring his senses.

A sudden movement from her drew his eyes to her lips, painted a soft pink, as she slowly dragged her tongue across them. A wink followed, so quick and mischievous that he might've imagined it, but for the cheeky grin that remained. A palpable jolt shot through him, his heart pounding an erratic rhythm against his chest.

Gritting his teeth, he fought to suppress the wave of desire that surged within him, his grip on the hockey stick tightening. Thoughts of her soft lips, of the light scent of vanilla that seemed to cling to her, and the fiery spirit that so often had him both irked and enchanted, threatened to drown him.

Evie was the coach's daughter, a truth that reverberated in his mind like a mantra and a warning. His gaze lingered a moment longer, tracing her fiery red hair that fell in loose waves over her shoulders, her small, almost petite frame that held a spirit far too fierce. And then, the reality of his situation—the injury, his future hanging in the balance, the unspoken rules of not crossing that particular line—rushed back in. "Earth to Crowe." Dominic's voice cut through his haze, bringing him back to the ice and the men around him. "We're heading to the locker room. You coming?"

Crowe nodded, casting one last glance toward the glass where Evie had been, her lingering presence still imprinted in the space. He forced a small, tight-lipped smile and followed his team off the ice. His mind, however, remained entrapped by a pair of lively green eyes and the taste of forbidden fruit.

PUCK AROUND AND FIND OUT

A short time later, the steam from the hot shower wrapped around Crowe like a comforting blanket, soothing his aching muscles and numbing the faint throbbing that still lingered in his injured limb. The sound of cascading water filled his ears, the rhythmic pulse a momentary escape from the chaos of the outside world.

As he turned off the water and stepped out, reaching for the rough-hewn towel hanging on a nearby hook, the muted voices of his teammates filtered through the dense fog of steam. A thick tension punctuated their words that caused a knot to form in Crowe's gut.

"Do you think Crowe still has it in him?" That was Carter, the new recruit. His voice carried a trace of worry that gnawed at Crowe's calm exterior.

There was a brief silence before Andrei, the Russian forward, said, his deep voice resonating in the confined space, "Is not easy, recovery. And age…is against him."

A low hum of agreement followed Andrei's statement, followed by Ty's solemn input. "He's not as fast as he used to be, that's for sure."

A heavy pause fell over the conversation, each man lost in their thoughts. The locker room, usually a place of camaraderie and post-game banter, felt more like a courtroom, with Crowe standing as the silent defendant.

He remained behind the thin partition, each word from his teammates a hammer blow, piercing through the veil of his recovery-induced optimism. His heart pounded heavily in his chest, fear and doubt seeping into his veins like poison.

His hand tightened around the towel, knuckles turning white with the force of his grip. Their words held a haunting truth, a mirror reflecting his inner turmoil and fears. He was older, slower, and recovery hadn't been as easy as he'd hoped. Could he still keep up? Or would he be left behind?

Steeling himself, he swallowed the lump in his throat. The whispers of doubt were impossible to ignore, but he was far from ready to give up.

Crowe was no stranger to challenges, and this was just another hurdle to overcome.

Silently, he dressed and exited the shower room, his features schooled into an expression of determination. His path lay riddled with doubt and uncertainty, but he knew only one way to go—forward.

Chapter 2: Coach's Daughter

The intoxicating blend of melted cheese, tangy tomato sauce, and fresh basil hung heavily in the air as Crowe entered the bustling pizzeria. It was a well-loved haunt for the team and a tradition to grab a slice or two after an exhausting practice. The friendly chatter of his teammates filled the room, the boisterous laughter and energetic banter bouncing off the graffiti-covered walls and vintage posters.

The soft, welcoming glow from the hanging lights above created a warm, homey atmosphere, a stark contrast to the icy rink they'd just left. As he navigated his way through the cluttered tables and the thrum of activity, a familiar face caught his attention.

Evie.

Her fiery red hair glowed like a beacon in the cozy dimness, her green eyes sparkling with mischief as she caught his gaze. A coy smile played on her lips, and she waved him over, her fingers twirling a strand of her hair. There was something irresistibly inviting about her, a magnetism he found hard to resist.

"Hey, Crowe." Her voice was a melody that danced through the clamor. A slice of pizza sat untouched in front of her, its aroma mingling with the vanilla scent that seemed to cling to her.

"Evie." He managed a small smile. Despite the riotous noise and activity around them, her presence brought a sense of calm, which was a paradox he couldn't quite comprehend.

She gestured toward the empty seat next to her, her eyes twinkling with an unreadable emotion. "Join me. The boys are too rowdy tonight."

Her playful tone tempted him, and against his better judgment, he slid into the vacant chair. The warmth of her proximity washed over him, and her radiant energy was almost palpable.

"I missed you. The rink wasn't the same without you." Her voice was barely above a whisper as her gaze fixed on his.

Her words, honest and sincere, tugged at his heart, stoking the flames of a desire he'd tried to smother. The heat of her body next to his, the soft giggle that escaped her lips, and the way her eyes seemed to light up every time she looked at him—it was all too much.

Yet, the reality of their situation loomed between them like an impassable chasm. He was too old, too damaged, and she was too young, too innocent. And she was the coach's daughter. Her youthful infatuation could ruin him. Ruin everything.

With a sigh, Crowe looked at Evie, her hopeful eyes staring back at him. "Evie," he said, his voice steady despite the whirlwind of emotions within him. "We can't..."

She cut him off with a laugh, a twinkle of mischief replacing the softness in her eyes. "Can't share a pizza? Relax, Crowe, I don't bite. Well...not unless you ask nicely."

As laughter bubbled from her lips, and the tension eased slightly. Yet, beneath the jests and the teasing banter, Crowe sensed the lingering danger of a line to which he was treading too closely. Evie was a temptation, and one he wasn't sure he could resist. For now, as the night grew darker and the pizzeria bustled around them, he chose to lose himself in her infectious laughter and the comforting aroma of pizza.

Evie picked up her slice of pizza, her delicate fingers gently folding it in half. A tiny dollop of sauce smeared onto her cheek as she took a bite, completely unaware of the mess she'd made. An unexpected wave of fondness washed over him. She was so disarmingly herself in this moment—vivacious, a little messy, and entirely endearing.

Before he realized what he was doing, he reached out, his thumb brushing away the smear of sauce from her cheek. The contact was electric, sending a jolt through his system, and causing his breath to hitch. The corners of her lips twitched upward into a sly grin as she captured his gaze.

"Always looking out for me, Crowe?" Her voice dropped an octave, a hint of flirtation lacing in her words.

He retracted his hand, a sense of self-awareness rushing back. He cleared his throat and nodded toward her untouched slice. "That's a crime, leaving pizza like that."

Her laughter chimed through the air, the sound sweet and inviting. It was a melody that Crowe could listen to forever, and he found himself getting lost in it. It was moments like these that made forgetting their circumstances almost too easy.

She took another bite of her pizza, a sigh of delight escaping her lips. "Mmm, heaven, and to think you were going to lecture me about the sanctity of pizza."

Their conversation flowed effortlessly, every topic from the latest hockey stats to her favorite music filling the air. Her gaze held his, challenging him, as a spark of amusement flaring within their emerald depths. "Speaking of sanctity, how do you feel about the sanctity of a college education?"

He quirked an eyebrow, the question catching him off guard. "It has its merits. Opens doors, broadens horizons...why do you ask?"

A hint of vulnerability flashed in her eyes, her playful demeanor faltering for a fraction of a second. "I've been thinking after my gap year...college might not be for me." His surprise must've been evident on his face, for she quickly rushed to explain, "I mean, I was going to, had the acceptance letters and all, but...it didn't feel right."

Her gaze drifted off, focused on a distant point beyond him, and her thoughts seemingly miles away. She twirled a loose curl around her finger, the red strand glowing under the dim lighting.

"I've decided to stick around and help Dad with the team until I figure things out. It's what I know, what I love." Her eyes met his, their sparkling green depths filled with a mixture of defiance and uncertainty.

Silence fell between them as Crowe processed her words. It was a bold move, straying off the beaten path, but if anyone could do it, it was Evie. Her spirit was like a wildfire—impossible to contain and full of an insatiable desire to forge her own path.

"I think that's brave," he said finally, his voice sincere. Warmth spread across his chest as her face lit up, a relieved smile gracing her lips. "You should do what feels right for you, and if that's being here with the team, then so be it."

Her gaze softened, gratitude replacing the earlier defiance. "Thank you," she said, reaching out to squeeze his hand.

His heart hammered in his chest, her touch sending an electrifying jolt through him. He glanced down at their intertwined fingers, his mind spinning with a whirlwind of thoughts. This was dangerous territory. The boundaries were blurring, and the lines they should never cross were fading. Yet as he sat there under the warm glow of the pizzeria lights, with Evie's radiant smile directed at him, he found himself sinking deeper into a world he wasn't sure he could ever escape.

Crowe held her gaze, a symphony of unspoken emotions playing out in their shared silence. He should have pulled away, established the distance they both knew was necessary, but her hand in his felt so right. A warmth radiated from their joined hands, seeping into his skin and wrapping around his heart.

"Helping out the coach, huh?" He finally broke the silence, leaning back into his chair, yet not breaking their physical contact. Her eyes danced with mirth as she nodded, squeezing his hand gently.

"Believe it or not, I can be useful. I've spent my whole life around this sport. Plus, it'll give me a chance to keep an eye on certain old players who might need some looking after."

The teasing glint in her eyes was back, and he found himself grinning in response. "Old, am I? I see how it is. You're just lacking experience, so you can't appreciate the advantages of being old."

Her teasing expression held a note of hunger as her gaze raked him. "I can definitely appreciate. Trust me."

Her laughter echoed through the room, a captivating sound that filled his senses. The moment, so disarmingly intimate, felt like a secret shared between just the two of them. The raucous laughter and chatter of their teammates was a distant hum, drowned out by the rhythmic melody of her voice and the steady thump of his heart.

Their banter continued, one playful jab leading to another. Yet, beneath the casual chatter, he sensed the shift in their dynamic. It was as though they had crossed an invisible line, moving from mere acquaintances to something more complex and dangerous.

Despite the warning bells ringing in his head, he got lost in the rhythm of their conversation, the sound of her laughter, and the electric touch of her hand in his. It was as if they were in their own little world, oblivious to the reality around them.

As the night began to draw to a close, Crowe glanced at Evie, her face glowing under the soft lights. She was so full of life, so radiant, that it was impossible not to get drawn in. Yet as much as he wanted to lose himself in her, he knew that the consequences could be devastating. For him. For her. For the team.

With a heavy heart, he gently untangled their hands, standing up to leave. "It's late," he said, the words feeling like shards of glass on his tongue.

She looked up at him, her eyes reflecting a hint of disappointment but understanding as well. "It is." As he turned to leave, she called out to him, her voice steady and sure. "This isn't over, Crowe."

Her words followed him into the cool night, wrapping around him like a promise and a challenge. It was a dangerous game they were playing, but as he stepped out into the darkness, he couldn't get over the feeling it was only just beginning.

Chapter 3: Skating on Thin Ice

Bundled in her winter jacket, Evie leaned against the chilled glass of the rink, her breath fogging up the clear pane as she watched the players glide across the icy surface. Among them, one figure stood out—Daniel Crowe. Even from this distance, his commanding presence was undeniable.

"Penny for your thoughts?" The gruff voice of her father, Coach Manning, broke into her reverie.

"Nothing, Dad. Just watching the practice," she said, her eyes not leaving Crowe. He was executing a drill, his movements precise and sure, and a testament to his years of experience.

"I see." He followed her gaze. "Crowe's got talent. He's a good player."

Evie smirked, her eyes twinkling with mischief. "Is that all he is? Just a good player?"

Her father chuckled, his eyes meeting hers. "What are you getting at, Evie?"

"Nothing, just..." She trailed off, her gaze softening as she watched Crowe, his jersey clinging to his sculpted figure, the beads of sweat shimmering on his skin under the stark white lights of the rink. "Just thinking about the game, Dad."

He hummed in response, his eyes suspicious but not pressing further. With a pat on her shoulder, he moved away, back to his coaching duties, leaving Evie alone with her thoughts.

Evie watched as Crowe skated over to the benches, taking a swig from his water bottle. His eyes met hers across the distance, his intense gaze holding her captive. Her heart thumped wildly in her chest as a heated blush crept up her neck.

It was the same every time their eyes met—a wordless communication like a shared secret. She relished the unspoken connection and the electricity that danced between them. It was a thrilling game, one she wasn't ready to give up yet.

With a final lingering look, she pushed off the glass, making her way over to the bench. "You're looking good out there, Crowe," she said, her tone light and teasing.

His head whipped around, the surprise in his eyes melting into a soft smile. "Thanks." The warmth in his voice sent a flutter through her heart. His gaze held hers, a silent promise that sent a shiver down her spine.

There it was again, that spark. As she walked away, leaving him staring after her, she knew she was one step closer to winning this game. After all, she was Evie Manning—and she always played to win.

Evie spent the rest of the practice performing her duties, supplying the players with water and towels, making sure they had what they needed. She sensed Crowe's gaze on her occasionally, and each time, it was like a jolt of energy.

When practice ended, she waited near the locker room door, carrying a stack of fresh towels. As the players streamed closer, she held her breath, anticipating his appearance. She heard their voices, a chorus of laughter and light-hearted teasing, the camaraderie evident even to an outsider. Then he was there, sweat-soaked and looking all the more rugged for it. His short brown hair stood up in damp tufts around his head, mussed by his helmet. It was sexy as fuck. He saw her standing by the door and paused, his green eyes meeting hers. His brow furrowed slightly, a hint of confusion or surprise—or something else—flickering across his face. "Hey." He reached out for a towel. Their fingers brushed for a moment, the brief contact igniting a flame within her. She smiled while her heart throbbed.

"Hey, Crowe," she said, her voice steady despite the excitement coursing through her veins. "Good practice?"

He nodded, wiping the sweat from his face. "Yeah, it was all right." He glanced at her again, his gaze lingering a little too long. Her heart fluttered in response.

"Great," she said, her tone a bit more breathless than she'd intended. She quickly gathered herself, smiling at him before moving on to the next task. "I'll see you at the pizza place tonight?"

Crowe paused, a soft smile tugging at his lips. "I wouldn't miss it."

Evie's heart soared. It was a small victory, but a victory, nonetheless. As she moved away, she couldn't help but glance back at him. He was watching her, his gaze steady and unwavering.

She was going to win this game. She was going to win Daniel Crowe.

***

A while later, Evie walked into the pizza joint, her heart racing with anticipation. She scanned the room, finally landing on the familiar figure at a corner table. She caught her breath at the sight of him, his casual attire somehow making him look even handsomer.

"Hi." She slid into the seat across from him. His eyes lit up at her arrival, a small smile gracing his lips.

"He pushed a plate toward her. "Got your favorite."

She looked down to see a slice of margherita pizza, her usual order.

"You remembered," she said, surprised and delighted at the gesture. He merely shrugged, his eyes holding a hint of amusement.

Dinner was filled with light-hearted banter, with Evie playfully needling Crowe about his older age and supposed lack of knowledge about current trends. "I bet you don't even know what TikTok is," she said, trying to bait him into responding to her sass.

Crowe raised an eyebrow, amusement dancing in his eyes. "Of course, I know. It's that clock sound, right?" he said, his tone deadpan, making Evie burst into giggles.

Her laughter filled the room, and she saw something in Crowe's eyes—a spark of something she couldn't quite place but hoped was desire. She reached over and gently bumped his shoulder, maintaining the physical connection. "You're so out of touch, old man."

Crowe chuckled, not refuting her claims. Instead, his gaze softened, and he reached over, gently tucking a loose strand of hair behind her ear. The contact made her gasp softly, since his touch was gentle yet thrilling.

Their eyes locked, and she knew she'd made progress. There was something there, something more than just camaraderie or friendship. She could see it in his eyes and feel it in the way he looked at her. She just had to push a little harder to make him see what she saw.

She leaned in a little closer, her voice dropping to a whisper. "Admit it, Crowe," she whispered, her breath fanning across his face, "You want me."

He froze, his gaze piercing. For a moment, she thought he might pull away, but then his eyes softened, and he let out a soft sigh. "Evie..."

His response was interrupted by the arrival of their pizzas, but the moment had been enough. She'd seen it in his eyes—the desire and the longing. She'd managed to shake him and make him question his own resolve.

***

Crowe watched Evie from across the table, her youthful exuberance a stark contrast to his world-weary experience. She chatted animatedly about her day, her laughter filling the pizzeria, and he was captivated by her spirit. She was a whirlwind, this girl, so full of sass and spunk, and a spark that seemed ready to set the world on fire.

Her playful jabs about his age and supposed lack of knowledge about current trends made him chuckle. He allowed her the pleasure of seeing him at a loss, thoroughly enjoying her delighted laughter. Every tease and every bratty comment was a drop in a dangerous cocktail of desire and restraint that Crowe was trying hard not to consume.

As she playfully bumped his shoulder, the warmth of her touch seeped through his skin, a reminder of the magnetic pull against which he was continuously fighting. His hand moved of its own accord, tucking a loose strand of hair behind her ear. Her laughter subsided, replaced by a soft sigh as their eyes locked.

In the depths of her gaze, he saw his reflection—a man drawn to her, tempted and intrigued by the whirlwind that was Evie Manning. He saw the spark in her eyes, a silent challenge, an invitation. Her words rang clear in his mind, "Admit it, Crowe…You want me."

Caught off guard, he hesitated, torn between his heart and his head. His desire for her was palpable, growing with every passing moment, but his respect for Coach Manning, his worries about their age gap, and the potential damage it could cause his career kept him anchored. It was a thin thread of restraint against a tidal wave of longing.

"Pizzas are here." The waiter's timely arrival saved him from responding. He watched as Evie eagerly picked up a slice, her cheeks flushed as her eyes shone with the thrill of her small victory.

He spent the rest of the evening in her company, a mix of enjoyment and internal struggle. Every word she spoke, every glance she sent his way, tested his resolve, pushing the boundaries he'd set for himself.

Yet as he walked her to her car after dinner, he couldn't help but think, not for the first time, that Evie was something special. She was bright and brave, beautiful, and undeniably compelling. As he bid her goodnight, watching her drive away with a promise of next time, he knew, deep down, he was slowly losing this battle.

Chapter 4: Power Play

It was a charity event held at the stadium, the entire team, staff, and their families gathered to raise funds for a local children's hospital. Evie was the belle of the ball, her vibrant energy drawing people in as her laughter echoing across the room. Crowe watched her from a distance, a glass of whisky in his hand, the ice clinking softly as he swirled the amber liquid.

She approached him, a glass of sparkling water in her hand, her eyes glinting with mischief. "Playing the loner, Crowe?" she teased, standing close enough for him to smell her sweet perfume—a mix of vanilla and something floral he couldn't quite identify. He stiffened, aware of the many eyes on them.

"I'm not much for crowds," he said, keeping his gaze straight. Evie's laughter rippled through the air, the sound oddly soothing amidst the cacophony of chatter.

"That's not what I heard. I heard you used to be the life of the party." She stepped even closer, her arm brushing against his. His heart pounded in his chest, and his skin prickled where her touch had grazed him.

Crowe glanced at her, catching her eye. "And who told you that?" he asked, his voice barely above a whisper.

She shrugged nonchalantly, her eyes shining with amusement. "I have my sources." She stepped away then, tossing him a sassy smile before moving toward the crowd, leaving him standing alone with his heart racing.

Surrounded by a sea of bodies, all swathed in various shades of black-tie attire, Crowe found his eyes continually drawn toward the vibrant flash of Evie's bright red dress. She sparkled like a light in the crowd, , her laughter a buoyant melody that rose above the din.

"Crowe, enjoying yourself?" Elliot 'Tank' Jensen, their team's intimidating defenseman, nudged him with a grin.

"Crowded." His gaze still followed Evie's movement as she moved from one conversation to the next. He caught her gaze and a silent understanding passed between them, heightening the intensity of the moment.

There was a beat of silence before Tank broke into laughter. "That girl's got you wrapped around her finger, doesn't she?"

"Watch it," Crowe said, although his tone lacked real heat. It was challenging to summon annoyance when his attention kept straying back to the young woman who'd ensnared his thoughts.

Her overt flirtations and that contagious sparkle in her eyes were compelling, amplifying his already tumultuous feelings. More and more, he found his solid reasons against their involvement—his age, his career, the potential repercussions—being chipped away by the longing that swept over him every time their eyes met.

As the evening wound down, a slower song played, and couples began to fill the dance floor. From the corner of his eye, he noticed Evie walking toward him, an unreadable expression on her face.

"Dance with me, Crowe," she asked, offering her hand. It wasn't a question. His breath hitched at her proximity and the determination in her eyes. Caught in her pull, he set aside his drink, accepting her offer with a nod.

They moved slowly to the music, bodies close but not touching, their rhythm syncopated with the melody. The warmth radiating from her and the vanilla-floral scent of her perfume—everything served to blur the lines he'd been desperately trying to draw.

She moved closer, laying her head on his chest. Her arms wrapped around him, and he was holding her too intimately. Too visibly. Too close.

Too damned bad. For an incautious second, he abandoned all thought and savored the feel of her against him. She was perfect in his arms, as though made to fit. It was hard to let her go when the music ended.

The laughter, the warmth, and the dance—it all made for a dizzying cocktail of emotions, intoxicating yet disconcerting. Crowe was pulled into the whirlwind that was Evie, caught in the crossfire of her brazen flirtations and the realization they were sparking rumors.

As he glanced around once leaving the dance floor, he encountered curious glances and furtive whispers. An undercurrent of unease pricked at him. The reality of the situation dawned on him. This wasn't just a harmless crush anymore. It was a precarious situation that could implode at any time.

He did his best not to interact with her again, and the event ended soon afterward. With a terse nod to his departing teammates, Crowe decided to confront the issue at its root. The drive to Evie's place was filled with an odd mixture of apprehension and resolve. As he parked in front of her house, he took a moment to gather his thoughts, each one weighing heavier than the last.

Walking up to her door, he hesitated for a moment before knocking. As the door swung open, revealing Evie in her casual home attire, his worry deepened. His mind was a tumultuous storm of thoughts, but one thing was clear—they needed to talk.

"Evie," he said, his voice laced with a seriousness that seemed to surprise her, "We need to discuss what happened tonight." With those words hanging in the air, he stepped into her home, steeling himself for the conversation that was about to unfold.

It was a power play, and he was skating on thin ice. The question was, would he be able to navigate this treacherous path without damaging his career, their relationship, and his increasingly tenuous hold on his feelings for the coach's daughter?

Chapter 5: In the Penalty Box

The air inside Evie's home was thick with tension as Crowe shut the door behind him. He took a deep breath, trying to formulate the words he needed to say.

"You're young, you're vibrant, and you have your whole life ahead of you. And I…" He paused, rubbing his temples as if the right words were hiding somewhere in his mind. "I'm thirty-five and nursing an injury. This season might be my last."

Her brows furrowed, a clear sign of her confusion and frustration. "What does that have to do with anything?"

"It has everything to do with it." He struggled to keep his composure. He was a player on the ice, one bad season away from the end of his career, and she was the coach's daughter. The complications were self-evident.

"You're Van's daughter. That means something."

"So what?" she snapped, defiance flashing in her eyes. "I'm an adult. I can make my own decisions."

Before he could respond, she stepped into his space, her gaze never leaving his. The closeness was overwhelming, his senses filled with her—the sweet scent of her perfume, the spark in her eyes, and the pounding of her heart echoing his own.

He could no longer resist. With a groan of surrender, he pulled her into his arms and kissed her. He captured her lips with his, the taste of her momentarily driving away all his fears. It was reckless, it was dangerous, but it was also the rightest thing he'd ever done. The world outside ceased to exist as they lost themselves in each other, the heat of their bodies offering a respite from the biting cold of reality.

The penalty box was no place to be, but at that moment, Crowe couldn't think of anywhere else he'd rather be. His career, his reputation, his future—they all hung in the balance, and yet, the gravity of his predicament felt insignificant in the face of his burgeoning feelings for Evie.

Evie melted into him, her body responding to his every touch. Crowe's hands roamed over her curves and she shivered beneath his touch. He knew he shouldn't be doing this—he was a professional athlete with a lot to lose—but he couldn't help himself.

He needed her.

As their kiss deepened, Crowe's hands moved lower, down to the hem of long T-shirt. He tugged it up, baring her thighs and discovering she wore only panties beneath. He pulled away from her lips just long enough to take in the sight of her. Evie's skin was smooth and creamy, and he couldn't resist running his hands over it. "God, you're beautiful."

***

Evie's body buzzed with energy as she finally got a taste of Crowe. She'd waited so long for this, having loved him for as long as she could remember being aware of a man as a woman. His lips were rough and insistent against hers, and she felt her body responding to him in ways she never knew it could. And yet, amidst the passion and lust that surrounded them, she couldn't help a twinge of guilt. Their relationship was complicated, and her father would never approve of them being together.

Yet with Crowe's arms wrapped around her, she didn't care about what anyone else thought. All that mattered was the electricity that coursed between them, the heat of their bodies pressed together, and the pure, unbridled passion that consumed them both.

As he pulled away, she gasped for air, her cheeks flushed with desire. He looked at her with an intensity that made her heart skip a beat, and she knew she was in trouble, but she didn't care. She wanted him, more than anything she'd ever wanted before.

"Crowe," she whispered, her voice husky with desire. "I want you."

He didn't hesitate, pulling her closer. His hands roamed over her body, and she arched her back, giving him better access. His cock pressed against her, and a moan escaped her lips.

Crowe pushed her against the wall, his mouth exploring hers with urgency. His hands moved lower, cupping her bottom as he kissed her deeply. She gasped as he lifted her up, wrapping her legs around his waist as he carried her to the bedroom.

She was glad she'd tidied it for a change before leaving, but that was her last logical thought as Crowe laid her on the bed. Her hands trembled as she tugged at his shirt. "I want you so much. So badly. I've waited so long for this."

He cupped her face in his hands, taking her mouth in another punishing kiss. It demanded everything from her, giving her no chance to refuse. Not that she wanted to.

Crowe's hands moved lower, his fingers trailing over her skin, teasing her with anticipation. He unzipped her dress, letting it fall to the floor. She felt exposed, naked before him and yet, strangely empowered. His gaze raked over her body, and she flushed in delight, knowing he found her desirable.

"You've been such a brat." He said that sternly, but with a hint of affection.

She grinned up at him, unrepentant. "I had to make sure you noticed me."

"Oh, I noticed." His expression turned turbulent. "There's something you need…"

She panted with eagerness. "Give me everything."

He chuckled as he flexed his hand. A second later, he caressed the curve of her hip before urging her onto her stomach. She wore only her panties since he'd stripped off her T-shirt in the living room, and she wanted to shed them first, but his hand was insistent.

When she was on her stomach, her heart pulsing in her ears, he trailed his hand up her spine, stopping at her neck. His fingers massaged her tense muscles, and she relaxed under his touch.

"You've been teasing me for weeks, Evie," he said in a low voice, "And I think you deserve to be punished for that."

She drew in a sharp breath as he spoke, her body trembling with fear and anticipation. He suddenly spanked her hard, the exquisite pain sending electric shocks of pleasure coursing through her veins. His hand moved rhythmically between spanking and caressing, tantalizing her with waves of pleasure until she was gasping and pleading for him to intensify his touch, wild with desire and panting out desperate pleas for more.

Finally, when she was writhing with the sting of his hand against her sore bottom while her pussy spasmed, making her beg for release, he rolled her onto her back and moved between her legs.

She trembled as his mouth settled over her slit. His tongue explored her intimately, and her back arched in response. He lapped at her intimate areas, eliciting soft moans from deep within her throat. She dug her hands into the sheets beneath them as pleasure built up within her. He worked his tongue expertly, coaxing her closer and closer to orgasm.

Her fingers curled tighter as he slowly brought her closer and closer to the edge of climax until she thought she could take no more. She hovered on the edge for a second before realizing he was withdrawing.

"What are you...?"

"Together." The simple word, along with the way he shifted his body, transmitted his intentions as plainly as if he'd written a sonnet. She parted her lips and relaxed to ease his way. He slid his thick, hard cock inside her in one smooth, deep thrust. She gasped at the sudden intrusion, forced to accept him and accommodate his girth in seconds. It was delicious.

"You're so fucking tight, baby." He seemed to force the words through gritted teeth. "Could die happy now."

She gasped, arching her back as pleasure engulfed her. "Better not. Get me off first," she said with a semblance of teasing, though her brain was total mush right then.

He chuckled, and the sound reverberated through her whole body. Then, he quickened his pace, thrusting harder and faster as he drove her closer and closer to the edge. Her orgasm was building, the intensity of the pleasure threatening to overwhelm her. She clutched at his back, her nails digging into his skin.

He moved inside her with a primal intensity, and her whole body shook with the force of her orgasm. He didn't slow down. Instead, he kept thrusting, prolonging her climax until she thought she would go insane from the pleasure. Finally, he let out a loud groan and came, spilling himself inside her.

She laid beneath him, her body trembling as her mind spun from the intensity of her orgasm. Warmth spread from her pussy through the rest of her body, and every nerve ending was alive and tingling. The spasms of her sheath clenching around him must have been what he needed, because his cock stiffened even harder before twitching. A second later, the first jet of his cum hit her insides, and she moaned at the sensation. Another and another wave followed before he relaxed slightly, pressing his forehead against hers.

Crowe gathered her in his arms, and her body was still quaking with aftershocks. He kissed her forehead, the tenderness of the gesture completely at odds with the wildness of their lovemaking. She sighed and snuggled into him, feeling a deep sense of satisfaction. He had taken her to a place she had never been before, and she was still coming down from the high.

A frisson of delight shot through her. His body heat enveloped her, offering a soothing warmth that spread from the top of her head to the tips of her toes. The soft rhythm of his heartbeat against her ear sang a melody of comfort and safety, an irresistible lullaby that beckoned her further into his embrace.

Crowe's fingers moved tenderly over her back, tracing patterns on her skin. Each stroke ignited a fire that crackled and sparked beneath her skin, making her feel alive and cherished. His hand moved upward, weaving through her hair with gentleness that made her eyes burn. The tender touch stirred emotions she couldn't fully comprehend.

Leaning down, Crowe's lips brushed her forehead in a featherlight kiss that lingered, intensifying the intimacy of the moment. The faint scent of his aftershave filled her senses, a scent she was coming to associate with safety, warmth, and intense longing despite having just been sated in his arms.

His voice, barely a whisper, broke through her thoughts. "You're amazing," he murmured, his breath fanning over her face. His words, simple and honest, carried a weight that made her blink rapidly. There was profound sincerity in his voice, a truth that reflected in his eyes whenever he looked at her.

A surge of emotion welled within Evie, powerful and raw, making her heart pound like a war drum in her chest. The room was still, the hushed tones of their voices the only sound piercing the silence. The way he looked at her—like she was the only thing that mattered—stole her breath away.

"Evie," he whispered against her skin, the husky timber of his voice seeping into her, wrapping around her very being. His fingers traced an absent pattern on her arm, making her skin tingle where he touched. The word, her name, sounded different when he said it, charged with an intensity that echoed through her veins.

Caught in his gaze, she found herself drowning in the depths of his eyes, the warm brown reflecting a battle of emotions that matched her own—confusion, desire, and a hint of fear. More than anything, she saw longing, which was a mirror image of her own yearning.

Tentatively, she raised a hand, fingertips brushing his stubbled jaw, to trace the roughened skin with an almost reverent touch. The small action felt monumental, the world shrinking down to the two of them. And then he was kissing her again, lips soft and coaxing, a tender exploration that left her breathless. The world tilted, his taste, his scent, his touch, becoming all-consuming. The kiss deepened, and she clung to him, the outside world and the consequences of this moment forgotten. All that mattered was Crowe, and the torrent of feelings their kiss reignited.

Chapter 6: Scoring A Goal

Golden rays of dawn streamed through the narrow slits of the blinds, casting an ethereal glow in the bedroom. A new day had begun, ushering with it a sense of reality that the night had managed to keep at bay. Sleep-tousled and nestled against Crowe's chest, Evie traced a path down his muscled arm, her fingertips tingling with the heat radiating from his skin.

The world outside seemed distant as she savored the comforting rhythm of his steady heartbeat beneath her ear. The scent of him—a comforting blend of musk and sweat, a heady reminder of their night together—enveloped her. The sheets, rough against her bare skin, still held the warmth of their entwined bodies, a testament to their shared passion.

Crowe stirred beside her, his breath hitching slightly as he woke. His fingers, strong and gentle, found their way into her hair, his touch evoking a soft sigh from her. A comfortable silence settled between them, their quiet morning bubble unperturbed by the noise of the waking world.

Words hung in the air, unspoken yet palpable. Their actions from the night before, thrilling and unexpected, required discussion. She pressed a soft kiss to his chest, feeling the thud of his heart beneath her lips.

"We have to talk about this, don't we?" The words slipped out softly, laced with a touch of hesitation. Her fingers drew idle circles on his chest, tracing the contours of his muscles, her mind searching for the right words to say.

A low chuckle rumbled in his chest, the vibration sending a delightful shiver down her spine. His arm tightened around her, pulling her closer, his touch assuring. "Yes, we do, Evie." His voice, rough from sleep, sent a thrill through her. As she turned to face him, his eyes met hers, reflecting the same mix of anticipation and apprehension.

Her fingers grazed the stubble along his jaw, the rough texture sending jolts of awareness through her. His eyes, a deep hue of blue that reminded her of clear skies and endless seas, bore into hers with a silent promise of understanding and patience woven into his gaze. His arm, strong and solid, remained curled around her waist, an unspoken pledge of protection.

Words, heavy and profound, clung to her lips. Crowe's reassuring grip around her shoulder prompted her to voice her thoughts. "What happens next?"

Crowe's eyes darkened, the brilliant blue dimming as he considered her question. His hand, which had been idly playing with a lock of her hair, stilled. His gaze fell, focusing on something unseen as he prepared his response.

"I think..." He paused, swallowed, then looked back at her, his gaze steady and serious. "I think we have to keep this a secret. At least until the end of the season."

His words hung in the air, stark and heavy, their implications setting a chill in her heart. The warmth of their shared intimacy seemed to dissipate, replaced by a biting cold. Betrayal, sharp and biting, threatened to overwhelm her.

"Are you ashamed of me?" Her voice sounded small, distant even to her own ears. It was barely a whisper, but the hurt it carried echoed loud and clear in the silence of the room.

Crowe's gaze snapped back to her, surprise flickering across his features. "It's not that at all." His hand cupped her cheek, his thumb wiping away a stray tear that had slid down her face. "It's never about that. I would never be ashamed of you."

As he spoke, he pulled her closer, their bodies aligning in a comforting familiarity. He smelled of warmth and comfort, an olfactory reminder of their shared passion. Her hand splayed against his chest, feeling the rapid thump of his heart under her touch.

"It's my career." His voice was barely a whisper, carrying a weight of unspoken fears and concerns. "I'm not sure what will happen after this season, if there's even a place for me. And your father..." His words trailed off, the unspoken 'coach' hanging in the air.

His fears were palpable, resonating with a deep-rooted concern for his career, her reputation, and the future of their clandestine relationship.

It was a lot to take in, but as she listened to him, her initial hurt began to recede, replaced by a gradual understanding of the gravity of their situation. She found herself thinking about her father, the stern coach whose career hinged on the success of his team, and who wouldn't hesitate to cut Crowe from the roster if he or the team owner, Penelope, deemed him a liability.

The taste of reality was bitter, a stark contrast to the sweetness of the moments they had just shared. Yet, she couldn't ignore the truth. His career was hanging by a thread, made even more precarious by his healing injury and the ruthless nature of the sport. Their relationship, fresh and fragile, could cost him everything.

Her fingers traced the strong lines of his jaw, the stubble prickling her skin providing a tactile reminder of the man who had swiftly become the center of her world. Their eyes met, and in the depths of his blue gaze, she saw a mirrored understanding.

Slowly, she nodded, her heart pounding in her chest. His relief was evident, a tension leaving his body as he exhaled. His hand, warm and comforting, found hers, and their fingers intertwined in a silent promise.

"All right," she whispered, mustering a small, brave smile. "We'll keep it a secret...for now." The words tasted of promise and sacrifice, a vow made in the soft light of dawn that marked the beginning of their clandestine love.

***

The chilly interior of the practice rink, usually a welcome reprieve from the summer heat, was particularly biting. As Crowe skated, his breath fogged in front of him, disappearing quickly into the frosty air. His focus was off since his mind kept straying to the secret he was now carrying, the knowledge of his clandestine relationship with Evie a constant distraction.

He hardly noticed as the puck skidded past his stick, sliding harmlessly to the corner of the rink. The missed goal, an easy shot that he would usually make in his sleep, was glaring in its implications. His eyes caught Dom's, who'd been watching him with a concerned look.

"What's eating you, Crowe?" Dom's voice echoed in the cavernous practice rink, the usual banter replaced by genuine worry.

A part of Crowe longed to tell his friend, to share the burden of this secret. Dom had been his confidant for years, the one person he could count on to keep his secrets. Yet the gravity of this particular secret, the potential fallout if it were to be discovered, was too great. The risk to his career, to Evie, was too high.

He forced a laugh, his chest tightening as he skated toward Dom. "Missing a few easy goals, and suddenly you think I'm having a crisis?" He punched Dom lightly on the shoulder, hoping to deflect his friend's concern.

Feigning annoyance, Dom pushed him back, a playful glint returning to his eyes. "Fine, keep your secrets, old man."

His heart thumping in his chest, Crowe skated back to the center of the rink, Dom's laughter following him. This time, his aim was true, and the puck sailed into the net. He turned to Dom, a victorious grin on his face. As the laughter and friendly jabs resumed, Crowe pushed his worries to the back of his mind.

PUCK AROUND AND FIND OUT

In the confines of the locker room, the raucous laughter and animated discussions of his teammates surrounded Crowe, yet his mind seemed to float miles away. The scent of sweat and worn equipment, usually comforting in its familiarity, did nothing to anchor him in the present. Instead, his mind dwelled on the dangers lurking beneath the surface of his newfound happiness with Evie. Every whisper and every sidelong glance from his teammates sent a wave of paranoia washing over him. His mind was a battleground, torn between the yearning for openness and the stark realization of the potential fallout.

His gaze fell on his battered hockey gear, the worn skates and scuffed gloves a silent testament to the years of dedication to his career. The prospect of jeopardizing everything he'd worked so hard for at risk because of his clandestine relationship made his stomach churn with anxiety. He thought about Van, who would be pissed at him sleeping with his daughter. Then there was Penelope. If she thought he was harming the team in any way, her disapproval would be swift and harsh, cutting him without a second thought.

As he closed his locker, preparing to leave, the weight of his secret seemed to press down on him even more. The normally lively chatter of his teammates turned into a dull hum in his ears, their laughter echoing hollowly in the back of his mind. He grabbed his bag and headed for the exit, the cool breeze of the evening washing over him as he stepped outside.

The sight of his car, parked under the dimly lit lamp in the parking lot, sparked a faint smile on his face. There was someone waiting for him who would ease his burdens and chase away his fears. The thought of Evie, her smile radiant and welcoming, provided him with a sense of calm amidst the storm of his worries. He slid behind the wheel, his mind filled with anticipation of their impending meeting.

The drive to her place was a journey into tranquility, the chaos of his thoughts slowly dissipating with each passing mile. The warm glow of her house in the distance was a beacon, pulling him away from his worries and guiding him toward her. For now, his fears were silenced, replaced with the tender promise of shared moments and stolen kisses. He was on his way to Evie, and that was all that mattered.

Chapter 7: Offside

Crowe crouched low, his focus zeroing in on the puck as it spun on the icy surface. The frenzied roars of the crowd faded into a distant hum, his senses honed to the cool bite of the rink under his skates, the sour tang of sweat on his upper lip, and the sight of the puck whizzing toward the net.

The goal light flashed, red and triumphant, and the crowd exploded into cheers. His teammates swarmed him, slapping him on the back in celebration. It was their third consecutive win, each one hard-fought, with each victory sweeter than the last.

As the applause echoed around him, Crowe's gaze sought out one face among the sea of supporters. He found Evie in her usual spot, cheering enthusiastically for the team with the coach by her side. His chest tightened, her joy infectious even from a distance. A pang of guilt cut through the victory high, his secret with Evie a heavy shadow over the triumph of the evening.

Under the blinding flash of camera lights, Crowe faced a barrage of questions at the post-game press conference. His guard was up, with each inquiry feeling like a strategic probe, and each answer a measured maneuver to keep his secret concealed. A female reporter from a local sports channel leaned forward, her eyes bright and interested.

"Crowe, over here." Her tone overly familiar, "Your game has been on fire lately. Is there a special someone motivating this hot streak?"

The room filled with laughter. The question, seemingly innocent, ignited a flare of paranoia inside him. His eyes flickered toward Evie, who was standing by the edge of the room, a guarded expression on her face.

"No," he said, keeping his tone casual, "Just focusing on the game."

His gaze met Evie's, her eyes widening as the denial settled. The sting of hurt was unmistakable, her smile faltering before she quickly masked it with a nod. His heart clenched as he watched her step back, blending into the crowd, her cheerfulness replaced by a quiet reservation.

As he excused himself from the press, Crowe couldn't shake off the guilt gnawing at him. He'd hurt her by publicly denying their relationship. His secret was safe, but at what cost? The thrill of the win and the rush of success felt hollow compared to the guilt that washed over him.

The aftermath of the press conference hung heavy in the air as Crowe made his way back to the locker room. Each step echoed through the empty hallways, the silence amplifying his guilt. The smell of the rink still clung to him, the sharp scent of cold metal and stale sweat a stark contrast to the sweet aroma of Evie's perfume that he had come to associate with comfort. His heart pounded in sync with his quickening steps, the rhythm an insistent reminder of the mess he had just made.

Inside the locker room, the cheers and laughter of his teammates felt distant, their words fading into an unintelligible buzz. He found himself standing before his locker, staring at his reflection in the small mirror attached to the door. The face staring back was that of a man on the edge, his normally confident demeanor replaced by an unfamiliar worry.

Suddenly, the locker room felt too confined and the laughter too loud. He needed fresh air and space to clear his head. Stepping outside, Crowe inhaled deeply, letting the cool night air fill his lungs. The brightness of the stadium lights was dimmed by the inky night sky.

In the quiet solitude, he missed her. He missed the comforting sound of her laughter, the warmth of her touch, and the soothing lull of her voice. With every beat of his heart, her name echoed, a steady rhythm of longing and regret. He had hurt her, and he wasn't sure if he could fix it.

He lifted his gaze to the stars, their distant twinkle a silent reminder of the complex game he was now playing. His relationship with Evie had become a delicate balancing act, a series of calculated moves to protect their secret, all while wrestling with the threat of discovery.

His gaze remained riveted to the stars as his mind grappled with the tangled web of emotions. He thought back to the earlier practice session, where Dom had teased him about his missed goal. It would have been so easy to confide in his friend, yet the potential repercussions loomed like a menacing specter.

He craved Evie's comforting presence, her soothing words, her understanding eyes. Yet the very thought of facing her filled him with apprehension. His secret with Evie, so sweet in their shared moments, but so daunting in the harsh light of reality, had him skating on thin ice.

***

The familiar jingle of the pizzeria's doorbell announced Crowe's arrival when he entered almost an hour later. The scent of baking dough and simmering tomato sauce hit him as he stepped inside, immediately followed by the hum of laughter and chatter. His gaze instinctively sought out Evie among the crowd.

He spotted her at the pool table, engaged in a lively game with a few of their teammates. Her focus was on the cue ball, her brows furrowed in concentration. As she made her shot, the balls scattered with a satisfying clatter while her target sinking neatly into a corner pocket. A round of cheers erupted from their teammates, and her victory smile was infectious.

Crowe's heart gave a bittersweet tug. It was a familiar sight, one that had always brought him joy, but tonight, their unspoken distance cast a shadow over the warm scene. He approached the group, his greeting lost in the roar of the celebratory cheers.

Evie looked up at his approach, her smile faltering as she caught his gaze. Her eyes, usually welcoming, now held a guarded look. Her lips opened as if to say something, but she simply turned away, her focus returning to the pool table. The cold shoulder was clear, a silent reiteration of the hurt he had caused.

Crowe stood there, a soundless spectator amid the laughter and cheers. Evie's cold demeanor hit him harder than any check on the rink, her quiet reproach amplifying his guilt. As he watched her engage with their friends, her laughter ringing hollow in his ears, he wondered if he had scored an own goal in their game of love. He was dangerously offside, and he wasn't sure how long he could maintain his balance.

The laughter and chatter from the pool table faded into a distant hum, the joyous noise feeling alien to Crowe's melancholic thoughts. He made his way to the bar, the familiar chatter of the bartender offering a momentary distraction. His order for a slice of their usual pizza felt mechanical, the usually comforting aroma now holding a bitter reminder of his actions.

Moments later, he took his plate, where a hot slice sat, the cheese bubbling atop the tangy tomato sauce as a thin line of steam rose from its surface. Each bite tasted bland, the lingering guilt overshadowing the familiar flavors. His gaze flickered back toward the pool table, his heart aching as he watched Evie skillfully navigate the game. Her laughter and smiles were reserved for their teammates, with none spared for him.

A chime from his phone broke his brooding. It was a text from Dom, asking about their practice schedule for the next day. He responded with a quick 'yes' before setting aside his phone. The small action felt like a massive effort as the weight of his guilt turned each mundane task into an ordeal.

As he sat there nursing his beer and watching the woman he was falling for being distant, he felt a pang of longing. He wanted to go to her, to apologize and erase the hurt he'd caused, but he couldn't, not here in front of their friends. The cruel irony of his situation was not lost on him. The very secret that had brought them together was now driving a wedge between them.

The pizzeria started to thin out as the night wore on. His teammates dispersed, leaving him alone with his thoughts. His gaze lingered on the now-empty pool table, the echo of Evie's laughter still resonating in his ears. With a sigh, he stood up, leaving behind the half-eaten pizza slice and his hopes for a shared late-night meal. As he stepped out into the cold night, he realized scoring a goal in love was much harder than in the rink.

Chapter 8: Broken Defense

The arena was a whirlwind of pre-practice commotion with players engaged in warm-ups and equipment checks. Evie watched from the sidelines, her gaze locked on Crowe. He was skating with a vigor that felt forced, as if each stride was an overcompensation for the emotional distance he had been maintaining. The sight of him, so physically close yet emotionally miles apart, gnawed at her.

A cloud of doubt loomed over her, its weight pressing down. Was Crowe losing interest in her? Her heart pounded in her chest at the thought. As much as she understood the need for secrecy, the cold rejection was becoming too much to bear.

He must've sensed her eyes on him because he glanced up at her. His gaze was a guarded fortress, revealing nothing of his thoughts. He offered a quick nod before skating away, leaving her standing alone. A surge of hurt, frustration, and longing gripped her.

No more. She needed answers.

The moment practice was over, she cornered him by the locker room. He appeared surprised, quickly masking it with a thin veneer of nonchalance. "Evie?"

"We need to talk." Her voice was firm, the raw hurt ringing clear.

His face softened slightly. "Evie, later..."

"Now," she said, stopping him. "I need to know if you're losing interest in me."

The silence hung heavy between them. He looked at her, his gaze softening as his hands reached out to hold hers. His touch, once a source of comfort, now felt like a bittersweet reminder of their fading relationship.

"No, I'm not losing interest in you. It's just..." His words trailed off, a heavy sigh replacing them. He ran a hand through his hair in a gesture of frustration.

"Talk to me. Help me understand."

He took a deep breath, his voice barely above a whisper when he finally spoke. "Nothing has changed...my feelings for you, or the reason we have to keep this quiet." His gaze dropped, unable to meet hers.

Her heart constricted, her brain grappling with the weight of his words. Nothing had changed, and wis worries weren't unfounded. Her father and Penelope could be ruthless when it came to the team. She understood why Crowe felt the need to maintain distance, the secret of their relationship a dangerous threat to his career. She just hated it. It was harder than she'd ever imagined, especially when he'd denied a relationship when the reporter asked her loaded question.

"I understand, but I can't keep going like this," she said, her voice tinged with a quiet determination. His eyes searched hers as if trying to make sense of what she was saying. "I care about you," she confessed, her words shaking as they fought their way out, "Yet it's hurting too much to see you withdraw."

Her words hung heavily in the air between them. The unspoken implication was clear. She was reaching her breaking point. The cost of their secret relationship was becoming too high, the toll it was taking on her emotional well-being, too great.

He looked at her, his usual confidence replaced with a sadness that mirrored her own. "I... I didn't mean to hurt you," he murmured, his voice barely audible. He seemed to be grappling with his own emotions as if the reality of their situation hit him as hard as it had hit her.

"I understand we can't be open right now, but when will we ever be? Am I always going to be your...your dirty little secret?" The last words left her lips in a hushed whisper, as if saying them louder would make them realer.

Crowe winced at her words, his hand instinctively reaching out to her. She stepped back, her eyes flashing with a hurt defiance. "What if they don't renew your contract next year?" Her voice was rising now, her calm façade crumbling. "Or what if they do? How long will I have to hide in the shadows?"

Her words made him flinch. He was silent for a long moment, his gaze haunted. He looked as lost as she felt. "I...I don't know. I wish I had the answers. I don't want to hide you. You're not a secret to be ashamed of." His words were sincere, raw with emotion, yet they provided little comfort.

Evie took a deep breath, attempting to regain some composure. Her brain was a whirl of thoughts, but one stood out above the rest. She was young, and naïve maybe, but she'd always believed in working for what she wanted. And she wanted Crowe. Yet she also wanted more than secret dates and hushed whispers. She wanted to hold his hand in public, to cheer him on from the stands, and to be able to support him openly. "I care about you, even more than I thought I could when I dreamed of us together, but I also need to care about myself. I can't stay hidden forever."

Her voice was a mix of pleading and warning as she hoped he would understand. "I won't ask you to choose between me and your career. That's not fair. Yet I can't promise I'll keep waiting in the shadows."

His eyes were dark with pain as he nodded, understanding her predicament but clearly equally torn by his own. The tension between them was almost palpable, a painful static that marked the crossroads where they'd found themselves.

"I don't want to lose you," he said finally, his voice barely above a whisper.

Her heart was aching as she whispered back, " I don't want to lose myself."

When he didn't reply, she turned and walked away. As Evie left the ice complex, the chill of the night air bit through her clothing. She walked briskly, her heels clicking rhythmically against the asphalt, the sound a hollow echo of her chaotic thoughts.

Her apartment was a sanctuary, its familiar walls and warm lighting a comfort. Despite that, when she got home several minutes later, it felt stifling, with the silence amplifying her loneliness. She kicked off her shoes, her bare feet sinking into the plush carpet. She sank onto the couch, her mind replaying the conversation with Crowe.

She could still feel the warmth of his touch and see the pain in his eyes. His admission of not wanting to lose her lingered, the memory a sharp contrast to the bitter reality of their predicament. Evie didn't want to lose Crowe either, but the cost of their clandestine relationship was proving too steep.

Her thoughts swirled, a hurricane of emotions and questions. Amid the chaos, she felt a spark of clarity. She needed distance. To protect her heart and to salvage the shreds of her dignity, she needed to step back. For now, at least.

The decision wasn't easy. It felt like admitting defeat. Yet as she repeated it to herself, the words felt right. She needed to protect herself, to preserve her worth beyond being Crowe's secret. To guard her heart against the pain that had hit her when he'd denied her publicly. Her brain understood his reasoning, but her heart couldn't go along with it any longer.

Her phone buzzed, breaking the silence. She glanced at the screen, her heart sinking as she recognized Crowe's number. He was reaching out, trying to bridge the distance she had just decided to enforce. Her finger hovered over the 'accept' button with the lure of his voice a powerful temptation.

With a heavy heart, she let the call go unanswered. She turned off her phone, her resolve solidifying. The silence of her apartment returned, a deafening reminder of her decision. This was for the best, she reminded herself. She had to believe that, even if it didn't feel like it right now.

47

Chapter 9: Ice Out

The biting chill of the ice under his skates, a sensation that once thrilled him, now seemed to seep into his bones, amplifying his feeling of unease. Each pass of the puck felt hollow, every calculated maneuver met with a loss of focus. Crowe's game had dipped, and he felt the impact, both on and off the ice.

In the team's locker room, the atmosphere had shifted noticeably. Dom, normally full of easy banter, watched Crowe in silent concern. His other teammates also seemed to share the sentiment, their voices quieter and their laughter dimmed.

After a particularly grueling practice, Crowe caught his reflection in the mirror. His usually confident gaze was now shadowed with worry. He splashed water onto his face, trying to wash away the remnants of his stress.

"Hey, Crowe," Dom's voice echoed across the locker room, "You good, man?" His concern was palpable, even from a distance.

"Yeah," said Crowe, trying to infuse his voice with a confidence he didn't feel, "Just a rough patch."

Yet the rough patch felt like it was becoming a chasm, with each passing day widening the gap between him and his usual form. He found himself constantly checking his phone, and the lack of messages from Evie became a constant reminder of the distance between them that he didn't know would ever close.

One evening, he saw Evie at the usual pizza place, laughing and talking with some friends. His heart ached at the sight of her. She looked beautiful, her eyes shining with happiness he realized he hadn't seen in a while. Only looking closer did he see it was false happiness. She seemed as miserable as him. He yearned to talk to her, to bridge the distance, but her false laughter was a stark reminder of the wall between them.

The sight of her, so vibrant and alive, drove a painful thorn into his heart. He wanted to approach her, to call her name across the noisy restaurant, but he couldn't. He was a spectator in her life now, the distance between them an icy chasm that he couldn't seem to bridge.

As he stood there, rooted to the spot, a hand clapped on his shoulder. It was Dom, a furrow of concern etching his normally jovial face.

"You're looking at her like a lost puppy." Dom's voice was full of concern.

Crowe shot him a side glance before his eyes moved back to Evie, who was now engaged in an animated conversation with a fellow team member. "I messed up, Dom," he said, his voice barely a whisper.

Dom was silent for a moment before he patted Crowe's back in a gesture of silent support. "You'll figure it out," he said, his voice firm, "You always do."

Crowe gave a bitter chuckle. "This time, I'm not so sure."

Hours later, back at his apartment, the solitude loomed larger than ever. The cold, empty space echoed his feelings—loneliness, regret, and a deep longing for a connection he had pushed away. He picked up his phone several times, Evie's number at his fingertips, but he couldn't bring himself to call her. He knew she wouldn't pick up, and he was too raw to handle another rejection, no matter how small, in this fragile state of mind.

Later, during an early morning practice, the strain of his emotional turmoil began to seep into his performance on the ice. Each pass of the puck seemed clumsy, and every shot at the goal was off the mark. His coach, usually a man of few words, called him over.

Van eyed him with a stern frown. "You're one of the best players we have, even with your injury, but these past few games...you've been off. You need to sort it out."

Crowe nodded, but a storm brewed inside him. How could he sort it out? His heart was tangled up in knots, his mind was a battlefield of guilt and longing, and his performance on the ice was suffering. He was drowning, both on and off the ice, and he didn't know how to save himself.

***

The stadium lights shone brightly against the polished ice, casting long shadows that danced and twirled with each movement. Crowe found himself lost in his thoughts, his gaze unfocused and his mind still occupied with Evie. As he skated absentmindedly, the puck came hurtling toward him. He moved to intercept it, but his timing was off. The sudden imbalance caused him to falter just as Andrei was speeding toward him.

The impact was immediate and brutal. Crowe hit the ice hard, his knee twisting at an odd angle. A sharp stab of pain shot through him, followed by a deep, throbbing ache. His breath hitched in his throat as the world spun around him.

"Man down!" someone yelled, but the words seemed distant, echoing as if from the end of a long tunnel.

As the medical team rushed toward him, Crowe laid there on the ice, his knee throbbing in pain. The collision with Andrei was an accident, but it was one that could've been avoided if he'd been paying attention.

A few minutes later in the locker room, with an ice pack strapped to his knee, Crowe could barely meet the coach's stern gaze. Coach Van was a man of few words, but his disappointment was clear.

Coach Van's voice was low and steady. "I need you to get your head in the game. We can't afford mistakes like this."

"I understand, Coach," he said, trying to mask the pain in his voice.

"Go home and get some rest. We need you back on your feet." His tone softened slightly, "And sort whatever it is that's distracting you."

Crowe nodded, his mind swirling with the implications of his injury. His career was in jeopardy, his relationship with Evie was crumbling, and his emotions were in turmoil. As he hobbled out of the locker room, supported by Dom, he was spiraling into a dark abyss, unsure if he could claw his way out.

The days of rest turned out to be anything but restful. Each tick of the clock echoed in the quiet of his apartment, each passing minute bringing an amplified sense of isolation. His knee, though healing, was a constant reminder of his slip-up, his mind wandering back to the incident on the ice. The apartment felt too large, too silent, with each room a stark reminder of his solitude.

In the quiet, his thoughts invariably drifted to Evie. Her laughter echoed in his mind, her touch lingered on his skin, and her eyes haunted his dreams. The distance between them felt like a chasm that was widening with each passing day. His heart yearned for her, the hollow ache growing stronger with each beat. His thoughts of Evie, once a source of comfort, were now laced with regret and longing.

Late on the third night, as he sat on the couch, his gaze fell on an old photograph of him and Evie from before they'd become lovers. They were at the pizza place, their faces lit up with laughter, and the memory of their shared happiness pierced through his melancholy. In the stillness of the moment, a realization dawned on him, its intensity taking away his breath.

He was in love with Evie.

Crowe felt the truth of it reverberate through him as clear as a bell. His heart pounded with the realization, the rhythm of it syncing with him mouthing her name. His sanity, his heart, his ability to play—they all seemed intrinsically linked to Evie. He yearned to be with her, to bridge the gap that had grown between them. He knew what he needed to do.

Taking a deep breath to steady his racing heart, Crowe got up from the couch, the photo of him and Evie clutched tightly in his hand. A sense of purpose filled him, the realization of his love for Evie acting as a beacon guiding him through the turmoil of his emotions.

With each passing mile toward her apartment, his heart pounded louder in his chest. Uncertainty gnawed at him as the fear of rejection loomed large. Yet the thought of living without Evie, of continuing in this agonizing limbo, was far more terrifying.

Standing before her apartment door a while later, Crowe took a moment to collect his thoughts. His hand, slightly trembling, reached for the doorbell. The familiar chime sounded muffled, as if resonating through the thick curtain of his anxiety.

The door swung open, and there she was, standing in the soft light of her apartment, looking surprised to see him. Her eyes were wide, her lips slightly parted, and an unvoiced question lingering in the air between them.

"Crowe?" she asked, uncertainty coloring her tone. "What are you doing here?"

"I..." Crowe started before his voice faltered. His gaze fell on the photo still clenched in his hand. Drawing strength from their frozen smiles, he met her questioning gaze with a determination that surprised even him. "I had to see you," he said, his voice barely above a whisper. "I realized something important...something I should have realized a long time ago." When she didn't reply, he asked, "May I come in?"

Chapter 10: Shot On Goal

It felt like a mistake, but she couldn't keep herself from stepping back and gesturing him to enter. In the dim light of her apartment, Crowe seemed different. An earnest tension replaced the usual grace in his posture. His eyes bore into hers, an intense fire of determination burning within them.

"I can't keep going without you. Not being with you is affecting me on the ice and off it. Everywhere."

The pain in his voice struck a chord within her. A part of her yearned to comfort him, to ease his pain. Yet the bitter sting of hurt and need to protect herself from more remained. Her voice shook as her heart pounded against her ribcage. "What about your career and my father?"

Crowe's gaze softened, acceptance reflected in his eyes. "I've been thinking about that too," he said, the struggle evident in his voice. "I know what I said before, about needing to keep us a secret, but…"

"But what?" Evie prodded, her heart heavy with anticipation.

"I was wrong," Crowe finished, his gaze falling to the floor. "I thought I could manage it, but I can't. It's you, Evie. It's always been you. The fear of losing you is more threatening to me than any career risk."

His words rang loudly in the silent room, echoing the turmoil within her. She wanted to believe him, wanted to throw caution to the wind and dive back into their relationship, but the fear of getting hurt again lingered. "It's not that easy. You can't just dismiss your worries about your career, Penelope, and my father like they don't matter."

Crowe looked up at her, his eyes filled with a desperate resolve. "I know it won't be easy, but I can't lose you. I won't. I'll figure out a way."

She was silent for a moment, absorbing his words. They carried a promise. His sincerity was unmistakable, but so was the enormity of the challenges they were about to face. She took a deep breath, steeling herself. "And what if you can't?" she asked, her voice trembling. "What if you can't figure it out? What then?"

Crowe hesitated, his eyes meeting hers. "Then at least I'll have tried," he said quietly. "At least I won't regret not fighting for what matters most. You."

Tears welled in her eyes. His confession, heartfelt and genuine, pierced her defenses. She loved him. She missed him. Hearing him voice his commitment, his willingness to risk it all for their love, was more than she could resist.

With a shaky exhale, she stepped closer, her voice barely above a whisper. "I've missed you too. I love you, and I'm willing to take this risk with you."

His expression softened, relief washing over his features. "Thank you, Evie." He closed the gap between them. His arms wound around her in a comforting embrace. When his lips touched hers, it wasn't an unsure embrace—he kissed her deeply and with passionate intent.

She responded with an identical degree of eagerness. Their bond was unmistakable. The embrace seemed to last forever, neither one wanting for it to be interrupted or ending too soon. As their kiss deepened, the sensation became more and more intense until there was nothing left but pure, blissful love.

When they finally parted, they were both breathing heavily. "I've missed you," she said again. "It's been hard to sleep without you beside me."

Crowe groaned. "I don't think I've slept at all since I started pulling away. I'm sorry."

She still had reservations, but she put her fingers to his lips. "Shush. Let's move forward, not back, okay?" At his nod, her lips replaced her fingers, and she pushed her tongue into his mouth.

PUCK AROUND AND FIND OUT

The kiss was just as passionate and intense as the last and seemed to transport them beyond reality. Nothing in the world mattered except for each other. Their worries were forgotten, and their troubles melted away. All that remained was the sheer joy of being in each other's arms again.

When they finally broke apart, Crowe took her face in his hands and kissed her forehead before drawing her close and holding her tight. "I love you," he muttered into her hair.

Evie wrapped her arms around his neck. "I love you too," she said softly against his chest.

They quickly moved to her bedroom, where they both began to undress. He carefully removed his shirt and trousers while she pulled off her yoga pants and T-shirt.

She was lightheaded from anticipation and excitement as he stepped closer, eyes searching for any signs of hesitation. He must see only eagerness in abundance.

His hands reached out slowly toward hers, guiding them together into the bed sheets that smelled faintly like vanilla.

Evie's heart raced as their skin touched, sending shivers flowing through her body. She felt all the pain, worries, and troubles fade for that moment. As they moved together under the sheets, Evie saw a look in Crowe's eyes she had never seen before—one of pure and unconditional love.

His hands ravished her body, exploring its depths with passionate hunger. Her nipples beaded into tight points as he teased them between his thumb and forefinger. He delved lower, gripping her mound firmly as his fingers penetrated deep inside her welcoming warmth. His fingertips skillfully plied the delicate lips of her pussy with slow and tantalizingly circular motions that left her trembling.

His movements were slow and methodical, each stroke carrying her farther away from reality as pleasure began to course through her veins. She was getting closer to the edge with every thrust his fingers made into her pussy until she was practically trembling with anticipation, as if it were just barely beyond her reach. Then he withdrew ever so slightly, as if teasing her before fully letting go.

A rush of intense pleasure flooded through every inch of her being like never before—an explosive sensation that engulfed her in a cascade of sheer bliss. Tension and release coursed through her veins, and even for a few moments, iyt felt as if time had stopped.

As he continued to caress her with his gentle yet firm touch, goosebumps rose along her skin in blissful anticipation of another orgasm. His deep and steady breathing became like an anchor keeping her grounded as pleasure washed over her body in waves a second time. When he would have kept stroking, she broke their deep kiss and wiggled away. "My turn."

He looked intrigued. "Oh?"

Pushing him back so he laid on the bed, she knelt over him. Evie kissed a line down his torso from his nipples, licking and nibbling, but not leisurely. She wanted to make him feel as good as he'd made her feel, so when she reached his cock, took him into her mouth eagerly, letting out a soft moan as she did so.

"Oh..." He issued a low groan.

Her tongue danced around his delicate head before taking the entire shaft deep inside her throat, churning and massaging it with firm but gentle motions. He moaned in pleasure as she moved up and down the length of his hardening dick with expert skill.

Evie stroked her tongue down his shaft, her breath a teasing whisper against his hypersensitive flesh. He groaned and trembled beneath her skilled ministrations, each flick of her tongue and press of her lips making him tremble against her. She caressed and teased him eagerly, eliciting a gasp or a moan with every move she made. Each indication of his satisfaction pleased her because she gave it to him.

He needed to be teased the way he'd teased her. Crowe was naturally dominant, but she was the one in control right now, though she was on her knees, figuratively. In reality, she hovered over him as he laid on his back stroking her hair and bucking his hips.

She increased her pace, moving faster and faster, her tongue slipping around his shaft as he thrust against it. His hands tightened in her hair as she felt him pushing toward the edge. She built up more pressure with each thrusting motion, and eventually it was too much for him to bear. Just as he hovered on the cusp, she pulled back.

He scowled. "What the hell?"

She laughed, enjoying his response. "You started this game."

He looked unexpectedly serious. "It's no game, babe."

She still liked having an element of control, but she couldn't bring herself to continue teasing him. Eagerly, she took his cock in her mouth again, bringing it to the back of her throat as she caressed him with her cheeks and stroked his cock with her tongue.

She bobbed her head and sucked more forcefully as his cock swelled and twitched. Crowe let out a loud moan as his body shook with the force of his orgasm, and he buried his hands in her hair as he came undone.

Torrents of cum splashed against the back of her throat. She choked for a second but conquered the urge to withdraw. Seeing how much it pleased him, she swallowed every drop before pulling back.

She smiled in satisfaction, feeling triumphant she had been able to bring him such delight. She kissed along the length of his shaft and moved up to rest her head against his chest, content to remain there until they both recovered from the passionate encounter.

"That was amazing." He sounded breathless.

"Um hmm." She yawned. "I need a nap. I feel as old as you are." She nudged him lightly.

Crowe let out a sound of protest, but it was halfhearted and good-natured. He pulled her into his arms, and she soon drifted off to a more restful sleep than she'd enjoyed since they'd pulled away from each other for the past few weeks.

***

She woke to Crowe's tongue busy between her legs. He licked her slit enthusiastically, making her hips rocket upward before his lips curled around her clit. "Crowe..." She moaned, unable to say anything more.

His mouth searched, exploring every inch of tender flesh unhurriedly. His touch was gentle, barely there as his fingertips explored her inner folds. He circled the bundle of nerves at the top with precision while his lips and tongue teased her opening in a way that made her squirm with desire.

As she gasped in delight, he applied pressure to just the right places inside and around that drove shuddering waves of rapture through every limb until finally they crested into one exquisite climax. She found herself panting as if she had run a marathon but flush with satisfaction.

Before she'd had much chance to recover, his mouth was on hers, sharing her essence, as he kissed her with hunger. His tongue swept into her mouth, and in one swift move he had her pinned beneath his body. Crowe was all appetite as his hands roamed her curves hungrily. She felt the heat radiating from him, warming every inch of skin he touched. His cock pushing against her thigh promised untold delight to come as she wrapped her hand around him, eager for more.

He continued to explore her body, trailing fire as his lips caressed her neck and shoulders. She was acutely aware of him in every way, his breath hot against her skin and the weight of him pressing her ever so slightly into the mattress. His hands moved lower still, tracing circles around each hip before slipping between them once more.

She gasped as his fingers curled around her clit, stroking and teasing in perfect harmony. His mouth left hers to whisper sweet nothings against her ear, which sent tremors of pleasure throughout her entire being. She was about to explode with every movement he made as a fresh wave of pleasure flooded through her veins and propelled her ever closer to the brink of coming.

He continued to devour her mouth and lips, exploring with such intensity that she felt like she was going to faint from the sheer pleasure coursing through her body. Their lovemaking had reached a new level, and nothing before could compare to this moment.

He shifted his weight and moved to hover above her, their eyes meeting in a silent understanding. He trembled as he entered her slowly, inch by agonizingly slow inch until he was fully seated inside of her. He captured one of her hands in his own and entwined their fingers, peering deep into the depths of her soul as they moved together in perfect harmony.

The world around her seemed to stop spinning, and the stars lit up beautifully. Vibrant blue and yellow hues pulsed in time with their passionate embrace as she lost herself in his languid blue eyes. She felt his breath on her skin, building steadily until it was almost a frenzied pant. His intensity matched hers as they both clung desperately to one another, every movement pushing them closer and closer to an amazing peak.

The heat that had been simmering between them only grew more intense as they moved in harmony until she felt herself teetering on the edge of something incredible.

A shuddering release suddenly wrecked her as a wave of bliss crashed over her like an avalanche, and before she could catch her breath, as he reached his climax. His body stiffened and pulsed as wave after wave of pleasure flooded through him into her.

With each undulation of his cock, a feeling rose within her that went beyond physical sensation. It was like emotion itself being poured out into their connection. In that moment, she knew exactly how much he loved and desired to be with only her—not just for now but forever. He was hers.

Finally, after the moment had passed, they collapsed together in a sweaty heap of satisfaction. As their breathing began to slow, he pulled her close, and she nestled into his chest with a contented sigh.

She felt as though every part of her being had been opened by the experience. It was the most intimate physical connection ever, and in that moment she knew that nothing would ever come close to competing with it. Even their first time together hadn't been so amazing.

Chapter 11: The Power of the Puck

The icy morning air bit into Crowe's face as he made his way toward the rink, a stark contrast to the warm elation still humming in his veins. The quiet of the early morning provided him with a moment to relive last night's reconciliation with Evie, a memory that unfurled a sense of warmth and relief within him.

Stepping onto the ice, he felt a familiar thrill. His skates sliced smoothly across the surface, each turn and glide executed with an ease that was directly proportional to his lightened heart. His knee didn't even twinge, and the puck seemed to dance at his command, responding to his every touch with renewed energy.

The silence of the rink was interrupted by the arrival of his teammates. Dom skated up to him, a knowing grin plastered across his face. "Look who's back."

Crowe returned the grin, welcoming the return of their easy camaraderie. "Missed my face, did ya'?" He quipped, accepting the playful shove Dom sent his way.

Throughout practice, their banter continued, infusing their intense drills with levity and familiarity. The arena, which had recently felt like a battleground of internal turmoil, had once again become a place of brotherhood and adrenaline.

"Crowe, if you keep scoring like that, I might have to start calling you 'golden boy' instead of 'old boy,'" said Andrei, clapping him on the back as they took a break. Crowe could only laugh, the joy of his renewed performance mixing with the relief of the previous night's confession leaving him too mellow to get irked about anything.

After the practice, as they retreated to the locker room, the air buzzed with an energy that had been missing for days. The other players threw occasional glances his way, their expressions varying between relief and curiosity, but Crowe shrugged it off.

That set the tone for the new couple of weeks. While his days were filled with the camaraderie of the locker room and the exhilaration of the ice, his nights belonged to Evie. Their relationship had taken on a new quality, one of quiet desperation and profound intimacy. Despite the clandestine nature of their meetings, they managed to steal moments of normalcy together.

In the dimly lit living room of Evie's apartment one evening, they poured over takeout and shared stories from their day, their laughter filling the silence of the room. These moments of stolen solitude were their sanctuary, a haven where they could be themselves without the prying eyes of the world.

Yet as much as he cherished these moments, Crowe couldn't ignore the constant weight of their secret. Each hushed goodbye, each stolen kiss, and each coded message was a reminder of the precariousness of their situation.

One evening, as he looked at Evie's face illuminated by the soft glow of the television, he found himself wishing he could openly share his love for her with the world.

As they reclined on his worn-out couch, an action movie playing in the background, Crowe turned to look at Evie. Her eyes, reflecting the flickering light from the TV, held a softness that melted him from the inside. He felt an overwhelming urge to say the words that had been looming in his mind for the past few days.

"Evie," he said, breaking the comfortable silence that had settled between them.

She turned to look at him, her gaze questioning.

"I wish we didn't have to hide us," he confessed. His heart pounded in his chest as he revealed his deepest insecurity.

Evie looked at him for a moment, her eyes filled with an understanding that only amplified his feelings for her. She reached out, her hand finding his. "Me too," she whispered, "Yet for now, this is our reality. It's better to be secretly with you than apart. I think we both learned that the hard way."

He nodded, squeezing her hand as a silent promise. They fell back into their comfortable silence, the movie playing a forgotten background score to their intimate moment. Suddenly, a knock at the door shattered their tranquility. Crowe stiffened, his eyes wide as he looked at Evie. He wasn't expecting anyone.

He got up slowly, moving toward the door. As he swung it open, Dom's boisterous laugh filled his apartment. "Crowe, you gotta meet..." His voice trailed off as his gaze fell on Evie. His expression morphed into surprise, then understanding, and then a mischievous grin spread across his face.

Beside him, a tall, curly-haired woman shifted uncomfortably. "Am I interrupting something?" she asked, looking between Dom and the pair inside the apartment.

"No, Pammy, not at all," said Dom quickly, elbowing her gently. "Crowe, this is Pammy, my date. Pammy, this is Crowe, my best matc. She wanted to meet you."

Pammy beamed at him. "I've been watching you since I was a kid, Mr. Crowe."

Ouch. Crowe nodded at Pammy, offering a half-hearted smile. He looked back at Dom, his mind racing. Dom gave him a subtle wink before turning back to his date, his face showing no sign of the surprise visit's true impact. "Is that good enough, or do you want his autograph too?" He sounded carefree.

Yet the secret was out, at least to Dom. Crowe could only wonder what the morning would bring.

"Nice to meet you, Pammy," said Evie from the couch, her voice steady despite the surprise.

Pammy's eyes widened, clearly recognizing Evie. "You're Evie Manning." Her gaze shifted between Evie and Crowe with new understanding. "Your father..." She trailed off awkwardly.

"Yes, he's the general manager," Evie finished for her, her tone casual, as if they were discussing something as mundane as the weather.

Pammy looked like she wanted to ask more questions, her gaze flicking between Crowe and Evie, but Dom gave her arm a gentle squeeze. "We didn't mean to interrupt your evening," he said, a hint of an apology in his tone. "We'll clear out."

"My autograph—" Pammy broke off.

"I'll get him to sign something for you tomorrow," said Dom from the corner of his mouth. "I didn't expect him to be busy tonight."

"No problem, Dom," said Crowe, offering his friend a small nod of appreciation.

With a final uncertain glance in their direction, Dom and Pammy left the apartment. Crowe closed the door behind them and leaned against it, his mind buzzing with the implications of their surprise visit.

"Crowe?" Evie's voice cut through his whirl of thoughts, bringing him back to the present. He turned to look at her. In the soft glow of the TV light, she looked more beautiful than ever. Her calmness in the face of their exposed secret surprised him but also comforted him. It reminded him why he was willing to risk everything for her.

"Let's finish the movie," she suggested gently.

He nodded, sliding back onto the couch next to her. The events weighed heavily on his mind, and he stared at the screen without seeing the movie..

A few minutes later, she interrupted his thoughts. "You're thinking so loudly I can't hear the movie," said Evie in a teasing voice, though he detected the strain and worry she tried to hide.

He chuckled lightly at her comment, wrapping an arm around her and pulling her closer. "Sorry," he murmured, pressing a kiss to the top of her head. "Just processing everything."

He could feel her nod against his chest, her hand drawing absent patterns on his arm. "Dom's a good friend," she said after a moment, her voice thoughtful. "He's not going to cause trouble."

Crowe nodded, knowing she was right. Dom was more than just a teammate. He was a friend and someone Crowe trusted. He hoped Dom would understand their need for secrecy.

"Yet it's not just about Dom." Crowe stared at on the flickering images on the TV screen. "It's about what comes after. If his date—"

Evie was silent for a moment before answering. "We'll handle it," she said, her tone firm with conviction. "Whatever happens, we'll handle it together."

There was simplicity in her words, an unspoken promise that eased his anxieties. He drew her closer, pressing his lips against her forehead in a silent thank you.

"Let's focus on now," she said, her voice soft and comforting against his chest. "We'll cross that bridge when we come to it."

He nodded, pulling her even closer as they turned their attention back to the movie. No matter what happened, they had each other, and for Crowe, that was enough.

Chapter 12: The Final Period

The heady aroma of coffee filled the early morning air as Crowe stepped into the coffeehouse across the street from the rink. Dom was already waiting for him, a half-drank cup of coffee on the table in front of him.

"Thought you'd never show," said Dom, an easy grin on his face as Crowe joined him. "I guess it's hard to get out of bed at your age."

"Didn't have you pegged as an early bird." Crowe flagged down a server and placed his order.

For a while, they discussed their training routine, upcoming games, and the usual locker-room banter. He was aware of his friend carefully tiptoeing around the real reason Dom had asked to meet him for coffee before practice. As their coffees dwindled, Dom's demeanor changed. He leaned back in his chair, fixing Crowe with a scrutinizing gaze. "About last night...your secret's safe with me, mate. I told Pammy to zip it too."

A wave of relief washed over him, though he wasn't surprised by Dom's promise of silence. He nodded, offering a grateful smile. "Thanks, Dom. Means a lot."

Dom just shrugged, a smirk playing on his lips. "Just remember this next time I need a favor."

Their conversation turned back to safer waters after that, both leaving for the group practice a little while later. The practice was intense, with each of them pushing their limits, leaving their bodies slick with sweat and their muscles aching pleasantly.

Crowe's moves on the ice were fluid, and he was more in sync with his team and his own movements than ever before. Even Coach Van seemed pleased, which was a rare occurrence on its own.

As he was getting ready to leave, however, his phone started buzzing incessantly, pulling him out of his thoughts. The notifications were from different social media platforms, each with the same insinuation. He was hooking up with Evie.

A sense of dread filled him as he saw his teammates checking their phones, their expressions turning from surprise to understanding to shock in some cases. He looked at Dom, but Dom looked as shocked as him.

His mind raced, the joy of the successful practice replaced by fear anxiety for immediate crisis. It seemed Pammy wasn't as tight-lipped as Dom had believed. As he looked at his phone, the notifications growing with each passing second, he knew their secret was out.

The usually boisterous room fell into an uneasy silence as he made his way to his locker, the weight of their gazes almost tangible in the air.

Ry Collier, known for his inability to contain his curiosity, was the first to break the silence. "So, Crowe," he asked, his voice casual, but his eyes held an unmistakable glint of interest. "Anything you want to tell us?"

A few chuckles echoed around the room, but all eyes were on him.

Crowe shrugged, pulling off his jersey. "Not sure what you're talking about, Ry."

Kyle Jensen said, "Ry, leave it. It's Crowe's business."

Yet Ry was relentless. "Come on, Crowe. Social media is blowing up with your name all over it. Something about you and Evie Manning?"

Carter Nichols, the ambitious newcomer, was looking at him with wide eyes, while Ty Davis, the quiet goalie, gave him a sympathetic nod.

"It's true," Crowe finally admitted, deciding honesty was the best policy here. "Evie and I are seeing each other."

A chorus of various reactions filled the room. Ry looked satisfied while others looked surprised or impressed. Alex Grant, the hotshot forward, even whistled, clearly impressed. No one appeared shocked now.

Marcus Bennett, their captain, finally spoke, his voice cutting through the noise. "All right, all right. That's enough. This stays in the room, you hear? We're a team, and we've got each other's backs."

Crowe nodded, grateful for Marcus's intervention. Yet as the locker room slowly returned to its usual banter and camaraderie, he was uneasy. Their secret was out, and he had no idea how the world beyond the locker room would react.

Before Crowe could fully process everything, the locker room door burst open, revealing a fuming Coach Van. His usually composed face was flushed, and his sharp eyes were flashing with anger. The room fell silent as he marched in, all eyes following his path.

"Crowe," he barked, his voice echoing off the tiled walls, "My office. *Now*."

Crowe's heart pounded in his chest. He exchanged a quick glance with Dom before heaving himself up from the bench. There was a heavy feeling in his gut as he followed Coach Van out of the locker room and into the hallway leading to his office. A knot of dread tightened his stomach as Coach Van's office door closed behind them with a bang, further punctuating the gravity of the situation.

Crowe swallowed hard, trying to keep his own emotions in check. "Coach, I—"

"You want to tell me why I'm hearing about your love life from social media gossip?" he asked, his voice deceptively calm.

Crowe swallowed, steadying his nerves before he spoke. "I... didn't mean for it to come out this way, Coach."

Coach Van rounded on him. "You thought you'd just start hooking up with my daughter and I wouldn't find out?" His anger was palpable in the tightness of his voice. "What were you thinking, starting something with Evie? She's just a kid, for fuck's sake."

"Coach, it's not like that." Crowe kept his voice steady despite the storm raging in front of him. "I care about Evie. I respect her. This isn't some fling."

Coach Van was silent for a moment, his anger replaced by disbelief. "And you didn't think her being my daughter would be an issue? Or the fifteen-year age difference?"

"I understand why you're upset. We didn't plan for this. It just...happened, and I won't apologize for my feelings for Evie."

"You better think long and hard about what you're doing, Crowe," said Coach Van in a low, menacing tone, "Because you're not just playing with fire. You're risking your career, your reputation, and most importantly, my daughter's heart."

With that, he swept out of the room, leaving Crowe alone in his office, the words "my daughter's heart" ringing in his ears. The silence in the room was deafening as he processed the gravity of Coach Van's warning. The walls of the office, usually filled with the bustle and noise of hockey strategies and pre-game talks, suddenly felt suffocating.

He leaned heavily against the desk, staring at the spot where Coach Van had stood. His words were harsh, but not unjust. The reality of their relationship was complicated, laden with so many challenges that even thinking about them made Crowe's head spin.

And yet, as he thought about Evie, he would do anything to protect her. He might be playing with fire, but his feelings for her were real and as tangible as the solid ice of the rink. Yet with the world watching, every move scrutinized and dissected by the public eye, their secret was now a headline, their private affair a matter of public discussion.

He was risking his career, his reputation, but most importantly, he was risking Evie. She was in the eye of the storm now, her name associated with him, and her privacy breached. The realization hit him like a punch to the gut.

Crowe had to protect Evie, to shield her from the onslaught that was undoubtedly coming. With a new determination, he left Coach Van's office, ready to face whatever was to come. After all, this wasn't just about him anymore. It was about Evie too, and he would do anything for her.

73

Chapter 13: Overtime

Evie had always loved the quiet calm of the training complex, a stark contrast to the exhilarating energy of game nights. Yet today, the calm was disrupted by an unexpected flurry of activity. As she walked in, a swarm of reporters surrounded her, their cameras flashing as they fired off questions with an urgency that took her aback.

"Evie, is it true you're dating Daniel Crowe?"

"What about the age difference?"

"What does your father think about this?"

"Will the team owner cut him for fraternizing?"

"Did you pressure you into a sexual relationship?"

Their questions, relentless and intrusive, closed in on her. Her heart pounded in her chest as she tried to navigate through the chaos, her secret exposed and being dissected by the world.

After what felt like an eternity, she finally found sanctuary in her office, the door closing behind her with a reassuring thud. She leaned against it, her breath coming in short gasps as the gravity of the situation hit her.

Before she could process everything, her office door swung open, bumping into her. She moved aside as her father walked in, his usual indulgent smile for her replaced by a grim expression. Her heart sank as she looked at him. His disappointment was palpable.

"Is it true? You and Crowe?"

Evie swallowed, mustering the courage to meet his gaze. "Yes, Dad. It's true."

Coach Van was silent for a moment. When he spoke again, worry laced his voice. "Do you realize what you're getting yourself into? He's fifteen years older, and he's on my team. I never wanted to see you involved with a hockey player. It's all about playing for them—on and off the ice."

Evie nodded, acknowledging his concerns. "I know it's complicated, Dad. Yet we care about each other, and you know Crowe isn't like that. Maybe when he was younger—"

Her father snorted. "No maybe about it."

It stung to think of him being wild and sleeping with the hockey bunnies, but she pushed aside the twinge of pain. "That was before us. Before me. He's not going to betray me like that."

Her father sighed, pinching the bridge of his nose. "Evie, this isn't just about you and Crowe anymore. This has become a media circus. Your privacy, his career... everything's at risk."

He was right. The reporters outside were a testament to that. Yet as she thought of Crowe, her resolve strengthened. She wouldn't let fear or scandal dictate her choices.

"I can handle it, Dad. We both can. We just need some time to figure things out."

Her father looked at her for a long moment before nodding. "I hope you're right, because the clock is ticking, and you've just entered overtime." With those parting words, he left her alone in the office, the silence echoing his warning. He left the palpable cloud of his disapproval lingering behind him.

Evie sank into her chair, staring at the closed door. Her mind swirled with her father's words, the reporters' questions, and the fear of what was to come. She felt a sense of loss, not just for her privacy, but for the simple happiness she'd found with Crowe. Now, everything was complicated and under scrutiny.

She had to call Crowe. She needed to hear his voice and reassure herself they were in this together. She picked up her phone, her fingers hovering over his name before finally pressing the call button.

The phone rang a few times before Crowe picked up. "Evie," he said, his voice betraying a weariness that mirrored her own. "I guess you've heard…"

"Yeah," she interrupted, "I've heard. The reporters are outside, and they ambushed me as I came in. Then my dad stormed in…" She trailed off with a sigh.

"I'm sorry. I never wanted to expose you to this." His tone reflected his guilt.

Evie swallowed hard. "It's not your fault. We both knew this might happen."

There was silence on the other end of the line. "What do we do now?" Crowe asked finally, his voice filled with desperation Evie understood all too well.

She took a deep breath. "We stick together. We handle this like we agreed. Together."

There was a pause before Crowe responded. "Together," he echoed, his voice stronger now, resolute.

"Stay in your office," he said, his voice firm. "I'm coming to you."

Evie wanted to protest, to tell him that it was madness for him to trek across the complex amidst the media circus, but it would be futile. Crowe was as stubborn as she was, and she could hear the determination in his voice.

Barely five minutes had passed before there was a knock on her office door. When she called out permission to enter, the door swung open, and Crowe walked in, closing the door behind him.

His gaze met hers, his usually bright blue eyes dark with worry. He looked tired, and a weariness that made her heart ache replaced his usual energy.

He crossed the room to where she was sitting, pulling her into a hug. She melted into his embrace, burying her face into his chest as he held her tight. It was a moment of respite amidst the chaos, and a silent reassurance they were in this together.

"What a mess," said Crowe into her hair.

She pulled back slightly, looking up at him. "We'll get through this."

He looked at her for a moment, his gaze softening. "Yeah, we will."

"I think we need a plan," said Crowe, sinking into the chair across from Evie.

She gave him a small, rueful smile. "I was thinking the same thing."

They spent the next hour discussing their next steps, looking at every possible scenario. Crowe pulled up his social media accounts, showing Evie the flood of notifications, the rampant speculations, and the escalating drama. Evie, on the other hand, read out loud a barrage of messages from concerned friends and relatives. The reality of their situation was settling in.

Later, as they stepped into the rink, she sensed the shift in the atmosphere. Hushed whispers replaced the usual banter as his teammates stared at them for a long moment. Evie was uneasy as she met their gazes. Some were supportive, offering quiet nods, while a few seemed to avoid her gaze.

With a deep breath, Crowe met the curious gazes. "Like I said earlier, Evie and I are together, but we wanted to speak to you together." His voice was strong and steady, and she tightened her hold around his hand. The room filled with a variety of reactions, from stunned silence to supportive nods. No outright objections, for now.

"So if you have any questions you haven't already asked, spit them out," said Evie briskly, trying to hide her nervousness at the possible reactions.

"I got a question," said Liam.

She was surprised it came from the player known as Viking. He was normally quiet. "What's that?"

"How can you stand to look at this bum every morning forever?" He chuckled, which unleashed a round of laughs among the others.

The tension visibly lessened, and she grinned. "It's easy when you all are the alternative."

Ry clutched his chest. "You wound us, Evie."

She shrugged. "You can take it."

Ty cut through the joking, his tone stern but not unkind. "You better not let this distract you from the game, Crowe."

Alex said, "Hey, if it makes him score more goals, I say let's set him up on more dates."

"Sure, but only with me." She put her hands on her hips and glared at Alex.

"She's staking her claim," said Dom with a laugh.

A few chuckles filled the room, breaking the remaining tension. Crowe even managed a grin, clearly appreciative of the light-hearted comment. Marcus, the team captain, nodded at him. "Just make sure you handle this right, Crowe. We don't need any unnecessary drama."

Ryan smirked, leaning back in his chair. "Well, your game does seem stronger when you're with her," he said, looking at her and then Crowe with a twinkle in his eye. "I'd say you're his good luck charm, honey."

Evie blushed at that but squeezed Crowe's hand, her smile warm and genuine. They'd made the first step, and the team stood behind them just as Crowe had promised in her office.

Next, they had to face her father. Together. It was important to put on a united front. The walk to her dad's office was a tension-filled journey, the echoing steps in the corridor resonating with her pounding heart.

As they entered the office, Coach Van looked up from paperwork. His gaze shifted from Crowe to Evie and back again. He seemed to have calmed down since their earlier confrontation, but the storm in his eyes was still visible.

"Sit," he commanded, pointing to the chairs in front of his desk. The tone was stern, leaving no room for argument. Crowe and Evie obeyed without a word.

Van started, his tone grave as he glared at Crowe. "I'm not going to pretend I'm okay with this. She's my daughter and she's fifteen years younger than you."

"I understand. I want you to know I care about Evie deeply, like I said. My feelings for her are genuine."

Van shifted his gaze to Evie. "And you, young lady," he said, a hint of fatherly concern breaking through his gruff exterior, "You think you know what you're getting yourself into, but this kind of attention... It's not easy. It's not fair to you."

Evie met her father's gaze head-on. "I know it won't be easy, Dad, but I care about Crowe, and I'm willing to face whatever comes our way."

The room fell silent for a moment. Van leaned back in his chair, looking from Crowe to Evie and back again. "You'd better be sure about this, both of you, because once this storm hits, there's no going back."

The seriousness of his words hung in the air. Evie squeezed his hand in silent reassurance. "We're sure," they said in unison.

"And the storm has already hit, to use your analogy. Everyone knows," said Evie with quiet composure. She was still nervous about the firestorm of PR ahead of them, but she wasn't embarrassed.

Just as Van was about to respond, his phone rang, the sharp trill slicing through the tense silence. He glanced at the caller ID, and his eyes widened slightly, adding to the tension in the room.

"Penelope," he said. The single word made him stiffen, and Evie's stomach clenched. Her dad's gaze never left hers as he spoke to the team owner. "Yes... Right now... Okay."

He ended the call, setting down his phone with a resounding click. "Penelope wants to see us. Now."

Evie swallowed hard. This was it. The next hurdle. And judging by her father's expression, Penelope wasn't in a forgiving mood.

They stood up almost in sync, Crowe's hand instinctively going to the small of Evie's back, and she appreciated the silent show of support.

Stepping into Penelope Hamilton's expansive office felt like stepping into the lion's den. She sat behind a grand oak desk, her icy blue eyes studying them as they entered. Despite her small stature, she exuded a formidable presence, her reputation as a shrewd businesswoman preceding her.

"Have a seat," she commanded, her tone brusque. As they settled into the plush chairs opposite her, she said, "I suppose you know why you're here."

They shared a glance before Crowe said, "About the news—"

"News? Which station? All of them. Not to mention social media. " Penelope's tone was chilly. "This is a PR nightmare. You two are at the center."

Evie straightened in her chair, meeting Penelope's stare. "We understand the situation, Ms. Hamilton. It wasn't our intention for this to go public."

"Well, it has," said Penelope, her eyes narrowing, "And now we deal with it. I expect responsible and professional behavior from both of you. This organization cannot afford to be embroiled in your personal drama."

"We will." Crowe had a determined set to his jaw. "We're prepared to handle the consequences."

Penelope nodded, a hint of softness entering her eyes. "See to it that you do. This team is a family. We need unity now more than ever."

Evie leaned forward, her voice firm. "Our relationship won't negatively impact the team. That's a promise."

Penelope held their gaze for a moment longer before breaking off with a terse, "You're dismissed. I have a press statement to draft."

Stepping out of Penelope's office, Evie let out a pent-up breath. "That wasn't as bad as I thought."

"Me neither," said Crowe.

Her father sniffed. "She went easy on you. Pen must have a hidden streak or romance in her." He sounded annoyed by the thought. With a terse nod to them, he turned and walked away.

"Maybe she does," said Crowe, looking shocked by the idea.

Since Evie couldn't imagine the team owner having any kind of softness, she didn't agree. "I think she's just pragmatic."

"We'll give her no reason to regret her support."

She nodded her agreement and took his hand as they walked away from Penelope's office.

Chapter 14: Victory Lap

The first few days were the hardest. Everywhere Crowe turned, there were flashing cameras, aggressive reporters, and the constant buzz of whispers. He and Evie were at the center of a media maelstrom, and it felt like they were treading water in a sea of speculation, judgement, and outright hostility.

Coach Van was distant, his disapproval palpable in every meeting and every practice, even spilling over onto Evie. Crowe could feel the weight of his gaze and the sharp sting of his coldness. Yet despite the chill in their relationship, Crowe focused on the game. With every practice and every match, he worked harder, pushed himself farther, and ignored the off-field drama to channel all his energy into his performance.

And it paid off.

Crowe was playing at a level he had never reached before. His passes were sharper, his shots more accurate, and his control on the field almost uncanny. Every game he stepped into, he brought a vigor and dedication that seemed to surprise everyone, himself included. The team was doing well, and Crowe was playing a significant role in their success.

Even Van, with his hardened demeanor and unyielding disapproval, could not ignore the transformation. One day, after a particularly grueling match where Crowe had led the team to victory with a last-minute goal, Van pulled him aside.

"Crowe." The harshness in his tone had softened just a touch. "You've been playing well."

He met his gaze, surprised at the compliment, no matter how grudgingly given. "Thank you, Coach."

Van's eyes narrowed slightly, his stern exterior slipping back into place. "Don't let it go to your head. You're not bigger than the team."

"I know that, Coach. I'm not playing just for me. I'm playing for the team."

Van held his gaze for a moment longer before grunting and walking away. Crowe felt a flicker of satisfaction. It wasn't a full acceptance, but it was a start.

As the days turned into weeks, the media storm began to subside. The initial shock and curiosity faded, replaced by acceptance that Crowe and Evie were together. Their personal lives remained under scrutiny, but the fervor lessened. They were no longer front-page news, and only a semi-regular feature in the sports section from time to time on slow days.

After one long, draining practice, Crowe found Evie waiting for him, a thermos of coffee in her hands. He gratefully accepted the warm drink, settling down next to her on the bench.

"Things are starting to calm down," he said.

Evie nodded, taking a sip of her coffee. "It was bound to happen eventually. The world can only stay obsessed for so long."

Crowe chuckled lightly at that, his hand finding hers after he stripped off his gloves. "I'm just glad we weathered the storm."

Her fingers intertwined with his. "We did, didn't we?"

He really looked at her. Despite the stress of the past weeks, she still managed to smile, her spirit undimmed. He felt a surge of affection for her and a wave of certainty. They were meant to be together.

"I don't want you to think that all this...drama...has affected how I feel about you."

She turned to look at him, her eyes soft. "I never doubted it. I hope you know, it hasn't changed how I feel about you either, except to make me love you more to see you standing strong beside me."

His heart hammered in his chest as he leaned closer, pressing a soft kiss to her forehead. "I love you, Evie."

Her smile was all the answer he needed. "I love you too, Crowe."

In that moment, Crowe knew he wanted to spend the rest of his life with this woman. The thought was as comforting as it was surprising, and he tucked it away, a secret plan for the future. Yet for now, he was content to sit with her, their hands entwined as their hearts aligned, ready to face whatever came their way.

***

A couple of days later, with a deep breath, Crowe knocked on the door to Coach Van's office. The idea of asking for Evie's hand was still fresh in his mind, and he knew despite the tensions, he had to talk to her father first.

Van looked up as Crowe entered, his stern expression softening just a fraction. "Crowe," he acknowledged, gesturing to the seat opposite him. "What can I do for you?"

Crowe took a moment to gather his thoughts before speaking. "I... I wanted to talk to you about Evie."

Van's gaze immediately sharpened, his body language shifting to a more defensive posture. "What about Evie?" he asked, his tone icy. "You'd better not be changing your mind..."

Crowe swallowed, steeling himself. "I...I plan on asking her to marry me," he said, holding Van's gaze.

The room fell into silence as Van absorbed the news, his expression unreadable. "And you're here...to ask for my blessing?" he finally asked, his voice barely above a whisper.

"Yes, sir."

Van leaned back in his chair, rubbing a hand over his face. "Evie is my only child."

"I understand, Coach," Crowe said quickly. "That's why I'm here. I love her, and I want to do right by her. By both of you."

Van was silent for a moment longer, studying Crowe intently. Finally, he let out a long sigh. "I can't say I'm thrilled about this, but I can see you're serious. And I know Evie. She's happier with you than I've ever seen."

Crowe waited, hardly daring to breathe.

Van met his gaze, his eyes hard but not unkind. "If Evie says yes, if this is what she wants...then you have my blessing. Tentative as it may be."

Crowe nodded, relief flooding him. "Thank you, Coach."

"Don't thank me yet, Crowe," Van said, a hint of a warning in his tone. "This doesn't mean I'm letting you off the hook. I'll be watching."

"I wouldn't expect any less, Coach," said Crowe. As he left Van's office, he grinned and pumped his fist in the air. It was a small victory, but it was a step in the right direction.

***

The restaurant was a symphony of golden lights and hushed conversations. Nestled in a private corner, a table for two stood bathed in the soft glow of candlelight. Crowe's heart pounded in his chest as he held Evie's hand, guiding her toward the table. She looked breathtaking, her dress accentuating her grace, her eyes sparkling with curiosity and delight.

"This is beautiful, Crowe." Evie's voice was barely above a whisper as she took in the elegant setting.

"Only the best for you," he said, his voice thick with emotion.

Evie gave him a quizzical look. "What's the occasion?" she asked, her tone betraying a hint of nervous anticipation.

Crowe merely smiled in response, gently pulling out her chair for her to sit. "Just wanted to show you how much I appreciate you," he said, his eyes never leaving hers.

As they settled into their seats, a waiter discreetly filled their glasses with champagne. The evening progressed at a languid pace, the courses coming and going, their conversation light and filled with laughter.

Yet, beneath it all, his nervous energy bubbled. He had planned this evening down to the last detail, but now, as the moment of truth approached, he felt a wave of uncertainty.

He watched Evie across the table, her laughter lighting up her face as her eyes met his with an unspoken understanding. She was his rock, his partner, and the woman who had stood by him when his world was falling apart. She deserved to know how much she meant to him.

Taking a deep breath, Crowe reached into his pocket and pulled out a small, velvet box. Evie's laughter trailed off, her eyes widening in surprise as she took in the sight.

"You're my world." The words were simple but conveyed everything he needed to say. He opened the box, revealing a delicate ring glinting under the soft candlelight. "You've become my everything," he continued, meeting her teary eyes. "And I want to spend the rest of my life showing you just how much you mean to me. Will you marry me?" The world around them seemed to hold its breath, the hum of conversation fading into the background. Then, breaking into the most radiant smile he had ever seen, Evie nodded, tears streaming down her face. "Yes, Crowe. Yes, I'll marry you."

As Crowe slid the ring onto her finger, relief and joy overwhelmed him. The challenges they had faced seemed insignificant in the face of their shared happiness. He was certain now, more than ever, that together they could face whatever the future had in store for them.

Chapter 15: The Winning Goal

As the final buzzer sounded, the crowd's deafening roar filled the arena. Players collided in a flurry of equipment and jerseys, the clear ice quickly becoming a kaleidoscope of color and movement. Amidst the pandemonium, Crowe was a beacon, his joy illuminating the entire rink.

From her place in the stands, Evie watched, her heart pounding with the rhythm of victory. Crowe had done more than just play—he had led, he had inspired, and he had triumphed. His critical goals throughout the season had steered the team toward victory, a remarkable feat considering his age and past injuries.

The path to this point had been a tumultuous one. Their love, once a hidden secret, had faced the harsh glare of the public eye. Yet the trials and scrutiny had only reinforced their bond, transforming it into something unshakeable.

As the team converged at the center of the ice, Evie's eyes remained fixed on Crowe. His helmet had been discarded, revealing the pure elation on his face. Their gazes met across the crowded stadium, a silent exchange that said more than words ever could.

As the echoes of victory chants filled the arena, Evie's heart swelled with a profound sense of peace and contentment. Their love story, like the game that night, was marked by perseverance, passion, and the thrill of winning.

Evie found herself drawn to the ice, weaving through the waves of jubilant fans and ecstatic players. Her pulse pounded in rhythm with the cheers and chants, but her focus remained on Crowe.

The thrumming energy of the arena around her seemed to fade as she neared him, her excitement at being near him as palpable as the first time she'd seen him on the ice when she'd been far too young for him to ever look at twice.

His gaze found hers as she approached, a grin breaking across his face. It was broad and joyous. It was a look she'd come to cherish as it was reserved just for her. "Crowe," she called over the noise, coming to a stop in front of him.

"Evie," he said, his voice a heady mix of exhaustion and exhilaration. He reached out to her, pulling her into a bone-crushing hug that spoke volumes about the intensity of his feelings.

When he finally pulled back, the question that had been lingering in her mind slipped out. "Are you ready now? To get married, I mean. Now that the season is over."

He looked at her, the love in his eyes plain as day, a softness to his smile that made her heart flutter. "I've been ready, Evie," he said simply, his voice resolute, leaving no room for doubt. "I've been ready since the moment I surrendered to what I was feeling. So, yes. Let's get married."

***

The day was already warm, though it was only mid-May. The hot Oklahoma sun beat down on Evie as she walked down the aisle clutching Van's arm. With soft green grass beneath her feet, she leaned slightly toward Van, whispering. "Dad, are you really okay with this?"

Van looked down at his daughter, a soft smile on his face. "I've seen him fight for you, Evie. I've seen him fight for his career. Yet most importantly, I've seen him love you. And that's enough for me."

Her heart lighter, she smiled up at him as they neared the arch of white flowers marking the altar. Crowe was standing there, his gaze locked on her as his eyes shone with love and anticipation.

The officiant began, his voice carrying clearly in the open air. "Dearly beloved, we are gathered here today to celebrate the union of Evie and Crowe in holy matrimony…"

Evie's gaze never left Crowe's. As they finally stood in front of each other, he took her hands in his, his voice steady as he began his vows moments later.

"One night across pizza, I looked at you and realized you'd captivated me. I was never going to be able to fight what I felt, though I tried. I'm happy to have failed. I've loved you through the good times and the bad, through triumphs and trials. I promise to cherish you, respect you, and love you for all the days of my life."

Tears shimmered in Evie's eyes as she responded, her voice soft but strong. "Crowe, you're my strength, my constant, and my heart. I've loved you since before I was supposedly old enough to do so, but that love has deepened and matured. I promise to stand by your side, to encourage you, and to love you unconditionally. You are my everything, and I'm so grateful to spend the rest of my life with you."

Several moments later, the officiant nodded, a gentle smile on his face. "With the power vested in me, I now pronounce you husband and wife. You may kiss the bride."

With that, Crowe pulled Evie into his arms, their kiss a seal to their promises, a testament to their enduring love under the bright May sun. The reception was in a beautifully decorated garden adjoining the ceremony site. Underneath a canopy of twinkling fairy lights that would fully come alive after dark, fresh flowers and delicate silverware adorned the tables. The atmosphere was jubilant, filled with laughter, music, and the clinking of glasses.

Crowe's hockey teammates were in high spirits, making the rounds with boisterous toasts. Alex stood up at one point, holding his champagne glass high. "To Crowe, the oldest player in the league, yet the fastest on the ice. May his marriage be as victorious as our last season." The crowd roared with laughter and applause, glasses raised in agreement.

A hush fell over the crowd as Dom rose to his feet. His usual playful demeanor was replaced by a solemnity that was rare for the lively player. "To Crowe," he said as he lifted his glass aloft. His voice echoed through the garden. "A brother on and off the ice. We've been through thick and thin together, through goals, injuries, and recovery. I've seen your struggles and your victories, and through it all, you've never lost your spirit."

He turned to Evie, his gaze softening. "And to Evie, the incredible woman who captured our grumpy old man's heart. Your presence in his life has brought out the best in him, and for that, we're all grateful." He raised his glass. "To love, resilience, and a shared future."

The crowd erupted in applause and cheers, the garden buzzing with goodwill and camaraderie. As the evening wore on, the garden was filled with music and merriment. It was a night of celebration, of love and friendship.

Crowe and Evie's first dance was beautiful. They moved with a shared rhythm, their bodies swaying gracefully to the slow melody. Their eyes were locked on each other as the world faded into the background.

As the applause and cheering erupted around them, they stepped away from the dance floor, preparing for their departure. Evie looked at Crowe, a knowing twinkle in her eye. "So, are you ready for another hockey season, Crowe?" she asked, a teasing smile playing on her lips.

Crowe blinked at her, clearly surprised. "How did you...?" He broke off, chuckling. "Penelope told you, didn't she?"

Evie laughed, her eyes sparkling with joy. "She might've let it slip, yes."

He looked disappointed for a moment. "I'd planned to tell you myself."

She patted his tuxedo-clad arm. "I know. Don't hold it against Penelope. I think she wanted me to be sure you had a secure future."

"I'm not angry." He grinned. "In fact, I'm excited."

She tilted her head. "About what?"

"Our honeymoon. Two weeks with just you in Aruba sounds way better than any hockey game."

With a playful roll of her eyes, Evie linked her arm through his. "That's what you should've said from the start," she teased, her laughter fading into the warm Oklahoma night.

A couple of hours later, as they walked toward the waiting car, she rested her head on his shoulder, her heart echoing the rhythm of their intertwined steps. She was married to her best friend, embarking on a new journey with the man she loved. Despite all the hurdles they'd faced, their love had prevailed.

And as they waved goodbye to their cheering friends and family, disappearing into the balmy night, they were more than just a newlywed couple. They were two halves of a whole, ready to face whatever the future might bring, together. Their story was not ending, but rather, just beginning.

Epilogue: Off-Ice Timeout

Crowe's heart was pounding as Evie walked toward him, her sun-kissed skin glowing under the moonlight. They were in Aruba on their honeymoon and staying in a private villa with a private beach. The sound of the waves crashing against the shore was the only noise in the air as they stood alone, staring into each other's eyes.

Without a word, Evie wrapped her arms around his neck and pulled him into a deep kiss. Crowe's hands found their way to her waist, pulling her in close as their tongues danced together in a sensual tango. Heat grew between them as they continued to kiss, their bodies pressed tightly together.

As their lips parted, Evie took his hand and led him toward the beach, the sand warm under their feet. They found a clearing where they could see the stars overhead, and Evie spread a blanket before lying down on it, beckoning him to join her.

Crowe lowered himself down beside her, his body trembling with desire. He ran his fingers through her hair, gazing into her eyes as he whispered her name. She smiled at him, her eyes sparkling with love and desire.

Without a word, Crowe leaned down and captured her lips again, his hands roaming over her body. She moaned softly as he found her breasts, caressing them gently before moving down to her hips. Her body responded eagerly to his touch, her hips bucking against his as he continued to explore her.

With a growl of desire, Crowe pulled away from her and shed his swim briefs. Evie soon traced the contours of his chest and abs. He shuddered at her touch, his body aching for her.

Crowe reached down and moved his hands between her legs, feeling her pussy as she gasped in pleasure. He moved his fingers in slow circles, exploring her body as he teased her with a gentle rhythm. Evie's breaths grew heavier as she began to move her hips in time with his fingers, her body trembling with pleasure.

Crowe could feel himself on the brink of losing control, but he forced himself to slow down. He wanted to savor this moment with Evie, to make it last forever. And so, he kept up his gentle caresses, his fingers finding the perfect spot and teasing her until her body was wracked with pleasure. She cried out his name as she came, her orgasm shaking her body and sending waves of pleasure through Crowe.

Finally, with a satisfied sigh, Evie opened her eyes and looked up at him. Crowe couldn't help but smile, his heart swelling with love as he gazed at her. "Your turn," she said with a satisfied smirk.

"Just inside you. That's all I want." He lowered himself down, pushing his cock inside her velvety hot pussy as they both moaned in pleasure. "I could stay like this forever."

He began to move slowly, his hips in time with hers as he kissed her passionately. Evie wrapped her legs around him, urging him to go faster and deeper. Crowe complied, his thrusts becoming more urgent as his pleasure grew.

The stars above illuminated Crowe and Evie's love, each lost in the other as their passionate embrace became more fervent. With every kiss they shared, the intensity of their desire for each other seemed to increase exponentially until it was a raging inferno that threatened to consume them both.

And as the stars shone above them, Crowe and Evie moved together, their bodies intertwined as they reached the pinnacle of pleasure. Their hands entwined, each caressing the other's skin as they continued to move in perfect union. The intensity of their love was palpable.

Suddenly everything exploded around them, a crescendo of pleasure consuming them both as their bodies shook with bliss. Crowe shuddered with pleasure, his orgasm crashing through him like an electric wave as Evie continued to cry out his name in blissful ecstasy. The explosive climax left him gasping and trembling as Evie's pussy clenched tightly around him again, drawing out more of his cum.

He held her in his arms until their breathing had returned to normal. Eventually, Crowe rolled off Evie and onto his back, drawing her close so she could rest her head on his chest. He kissed the top of her head gently and said softly, "I love you."

"I love you too." Evie snuggled even closer into him, closing her eyes as she drifted off to sleep in the warmth of his embrace on their blanket in the sand. The night sky's canopy of stars couldn't compete with the light she brought into his life.

His heart was full. He loved this woman, and they would have a lifetime of love and happiness together. With that thought, Crowe closed his eyes and drifted off into a peaceful, contented sleep.